THE WITCH OF SONORA

ALSO BY JOHNNIE BERNHARD

Hannah and Ariela

A Good Girl

Sisters of the Undertow

How We Came to Be

THE WITCH OF SONORA

JOHNNIE BERNHARD

Stoney Creek Publishing

Stoney Creek Publishing
A Member of the Texas Book Consortium

Published by

Stoney Creek Publishing Group

StoneyCreekPublishing.com

ISBN: 978-1-965766-71-2
ISBN (ebook): 978-1-965766-72-9
Library of Congress Control Number: 2026905890

Cover design by Adrienne Smith

Printed in the United States

This novel is dedicated to the men and women of the United States Special Operations Forces, the tip of the spear, the quiet professionals, the bravest of the brave.

The battle line between good and evil runs through the heart of every man.

—ALEKSANDR SOLZHENITSYN

Acknowledgments

With gratitude to Mrs. Smithers, my seventh-grade Texas History teacher, who ignited a love for the history and culture of my native state in the early seventies.

CHAPTER ONE

Nocona Ketemoczy
Border Patrol Agent
Edwards County, Texas

My name comes from a dead language, the language of the Comanche. The language died because that was what progress demanded. And progress was nothing more than The Man with his big stick and a fat wallet.

A few forgotten Indians, dancing in their faded eagle feathers, still spoke the language on the federally mandated land of the Comanche Nation in Oklahoma. Festivals tried to recall the language when youth dressed in buffalo hide chanted the words of the Comanche Ghost Dance song. But here in Central Texas, where I was born, my father and I spoke those archaic words every day. Not as a remembrance but as the only way to speak with full meaning. The Comanche way was not dead to us.

My name, Nocona, means "wanderer." I don't know if the name made me who I am, or I became that man despite the name. As a Marine in Afghanistan, I wandered for years, not typically staying in any one place for long, until I returned to Texas to work as a border agent in Edwards County.

My father told me my name was spiritual, derived from The People. The Comanche of Texas were the last free band of Plains Indians to surrender to the Whites and be marched off to live out their days in disillusionment on a reservation. Like a language, people's history should mean something. Or it becomes lost, forgotten, and absolutely meaningless.

Since I was a kid, I've been a wanderer. That curiosity to see behind the veil has led me into few paradises and many private hells. But the need to look beyond what was obvious began in Mexico City when I was eleven years old and walked away from my family into the *Mercado de las Brujas*, the Witches Market.

We were there as a family, not on vacation but on a religious pilgrimage for my mother. A Mexican girl from San Antonio, she was raised on a Catholicism both mystical and superstitious. She believed in Saint Mary as well as Santa Muerte, but it would be Mary who would bring a cure for her breast cancer, so my faithful mother prayed.

That year my father took every sweaty penny he could beg, borrow, and steal and got my mother to Mexico City. Not that he believed in miracles but because he loved her. It wasn't a demonstrative love. It was a love made from hard times a man and a woman endured in a place without biracial niceties. We were half-breeds. Like the song Cher belted out in the seventies. The racist monikers got a bit more comical or crueler, depending on where I lived at the time. Wetback. Red Man. Kaw-Liga. You've heard the names. You get the idea how deep the shit was for an Indian.

My bloodline was like most Comanche. Whites, Mexicans, Mestizos, and other tribes mingled in our veins. The

Comanches stole and traded children and women throughout their borderless world from the Great Plains to as far south as Mexico. There was no racism when it came to taking other human beings. It was about survival for the tribe. With a nomadic lifestyle and the harsh physical labor of the Comanche women, miscarriages and infertility were the norm.

My father was an independent and proud man who worked on a horse ranch outside Bandera, Texas. He was a direct descendant of the Penateka Comanche Chief Ketemoczy, who signed a treaty in 1847 along the Pedernales River in Fredericksburg. It was the only treaty never broken between Whites and Indians. It forged a peace between the Comanche and the German settlers of nineteenth-century Texas. Unwavering once he gave his word, my father was like his people. I'd like to think I am the same type of man.

In 1988, my father gave his word to my mother about Mexico City, so she could pray at the Basilica of Our Lady of Guadalupe. My mother said she felt cured after that visit. I'm sure my father doubted her, but he indulged her optimism with a shopping trip to the Mercado Sonora. I remember my mother being happy to spend cash money in the tourist trap with vendor stalls of bullwhips, sombreros, and goatskin wine bags. My little sisters each got a thin white Mexican dress embroidered with flowers of orange, pink, and turquoise.

Farther back in the mercado, away from the tourists and vendors, was a shop for the voyeur and the mystic seeker, the Mercado de las Brujas. As a wanderer and a typical boy who hated shopping and being with my annoying sisters, I found my opportunity to escape.

I wandered from my parents on that day in 1988, an eleven-year-old who was both terrified and curious by what I saw. Voodoo dolls, the bodies of animal fetuses floating in broth in glass jars, clustered pieces of animal and human hair fastened to crucifixes and cloth dolls, things both undetectable and unimaginable—all for sale.

I stood in front of a display of icons of the Catholic Church, tiny saints of clay, as well as statues of Santa Muerte, the saint of death, who was represented as a female skeleton with a scale in one hand and a scythe in the other. My mother said she was a good saint who could deliver us safely to the after-life. She looked horrible to me! I moved quickly away from the little Santa Muerte statues. I continued to explore the maze of stalls until behind those stalls were small rooms, where people entered through many doors and openings covered with curtains and strings of plastic, colored beads.

I saw her sitting on a small stool when a tourist opened the closed curtain in front of me. The woman must have been a hundred years old, short with a sharp collarbone protruding from her thin dress. Behind her was a black witch's cauldron with bones and a hawk's claw in it. Candles in all sizes burned near the cauldron.

The tourist, a short, fat man, gave her money. She then began touching his hands while speaking. Her eyes remained closed the entire time.

It was an unknown language she spoke. I knew Spanish and Comanche. English was a given because of school, but the words she said were mysterious to me. I thought if I stepped closer to the man and the old woman, I could see what was really going on in there. That was a mistake.

I still haven't figured out if she saw me, heard me, maybe felt my presence, because she opened her eyes and looked directly at me. I didn't know at the time what the milky discol-oration of her eyes was. Later I learned it was caused by cataracts. She stared at me and mumbled. A horrible smell came out of her mouth and filled the enclosed area, making my eyes water and causing me to gasp for air.

The tourist who had been sitting in front of her turned around and looked at me. He then ran from the stall, crying out, "Saint Michael, the arch Archangel, defend us in battle! Protect us from the wickedness and snares of the devil!"

I ran closely behind him, afraid to tell my mother and father what I heard and saw. My mother had whipped me with my dad's belt when she found me playing with a Ouija board the neighbor kid had. "Don't open the door to unclean spirits," she said. I hated to think what she would do to me if I told her I went into the Mercado de las Brujas.

To this day, I've kept my secret about the Witch of Sonora. She has followed me throughout my life. Those same milky eyes, the mumbled words, the woman in the thin dress with the protruding collarbone that poked through the fabric. I wasn't crazy. The Witch of Sonora was as real as the hand in front of my face.

I saw her the morning we flew out of Mexico City. I looked from the tiny plane window, and there she was running alongside the plane. I looked at my little sister sitting next to me, wondering if she saw the same strange sight. She only looked up at me then returned to reading her book. At that moment, I knew only I could see the witch.

From the boy I was to the man I've become at forty-five, the Witch of Sonora has followed me. Her sudden appearance is always frightening and prophetic.

The next time I saw the old witch was a few years later. She was sitting next to my mother's bed when the hospice nurse gave her the first injection of morphine. Some years later, I saw the old witch again when my best friend in high school flipped his truck on a farm-to-market road outside town and severed one of his arms between the steering wheel and broken windshield. When I served in the Marines, I saw her in the desperate crowd at the Kabul International Airport, when I was on the last plane headed home, leaving a failed mission and returning Afghanistan to the Stone Age. Each time she would stare at me either laughing or mumbling, filling me with dread for the horror to come.

This morning, when the moon was visible next to the morning sun, I saw the old witch on my way to work. The same relentless hag with the milky eyes leaning against the entrance door to the Kingburger on North State Street. And I knew, just as I knew when I was an eleven-year-old boy watching her at the Mercado de las Brujas in Mexico City, she was an evil omen that could never mean anything good for me or for the ones I loved.

CHAPTER TWO

Hannah Durand
Casa de Katia
Rocksprings, Texas

I've walked this land as a bride, mother, and widow. The seasons of a woman's life are as everchanging as nature, much like October easing its chill over the hot Texas land. I've accepted most of it.

I've cried hard and shaken my fist at God when I lost what I loved, only to turn around and fight for this place and my independence. I never gave in. Quitting was never part of my nature. It was the reason why I've refused to let people tell me how to live. Casa de Katia was evidence I knew what I was doing at seventy-three. That fact hasn't changed now that I'm eighty-two.

I got six girls living behind my house, eating three meals a day, riding horses on the ranch, and sleeping in clean sheets each night. Six girls, among the hundreds of girls we've served, were off the streets, safe from monsters. They stood, all six of 'em, carving pumpkins into jack-o'-lanterns at my kitchen table. Something many children were doing this time of year. These girls were living a normal life now.

Watering the garden this morning, I clearly remembered the day I started planting roses in memory of August, Buddy, and Katia. For my late husband, August, I planted a red rose bush, the Lover's Rose. A good man until the day he died; he was the love of my life. I planted the Yellow Rose of Texas for my brother, Buddy. He was a wild cowboy in his younger days, but he always made time for his little sister. For Katia, the little Mexican girl I only heard stories about, I planted the Ballerina Rose, so I would always remember the frailty of life, especially for the young who are taken from this world far too soon and violently.

In that one terrible year, I suffered those losses. I lost my sweet girl, Abby, that same year. A good dog can't be replaced, but I finally found June a few years ago at the Kerrville animal shelter. A sleepy mixed breed, June had become a favorite among the girls. I watched her sleeping under August's pecan tree earlier this morning and smiled. She had to be good with the horses to be a part of the family, and that lesson was a quick one for her. She and Rusty Bucket, my brother's cat, spent a lot of time together on the porch and in the shade of a tree. Jack, a highly energized Lab, joined us a few months after my brother died. Jack, unlike June and Rusty, stood alone. He patrolled the house, land, and just about everyone who stepped foot out here. He was our protector and my true companion throughout the passing days.

People often say life goes on and what doesn't kill you will make you stronger. I've thought about that for years with the exception that we always have a choice on how we're going to handle what life throws at us. My choice was to keep living, not just existing, after I buried my husband. I still ached for that man, mourning the empty side of the bed he once slept on every single night. But those girls living behind me needed me, and I needed them. I could hear their laughter from the kitchen while I worked the soil in the garden. To be loved and to have a purpose in this life was everything that made it worth living. I still had a reason to walk this Earth.

I turned the water hose off and dragged it behind the house. Elizabeth's truck was making its way to the gravel lot near the barn. I waved at her. I've known her all my life, from the time she was sixteen years old, pregnant and a bride. Her husband, Joseph, helped August and me for years out here, managing the land and animals. There was a time I didn't think we'd ever talk to each other—trouble like that can only be from a husband looking at other women. I didn't fall for it, and Joseph went back to his wife.

She came to work for Casa de Katia shortly afterwards. Elizabeth was a hard worker, and because of that, the shelter was successful. Our friendship, like most friendships between women when a man works his way between them, became cordial over time. Not too friendly, just polite. Sometimes a distant politeness is the best you could hope for between hurt women.

My cell phone buzzed in my pocket and shook me back to the present. It wasn't quite eight this morning, but that didn't mean anything on a Monday. Things moved quickly out here with girls coming and going from Casa de Katia.

"Hannah, it's Harold. I got some hard news for you."

"I'm just walking back to the house. Are you okay? I'm not sure I can handle hard news right now, especially this early in the morning."

Jack came running to my side, sensing something was wrong. I've always known dogs to be more perceptive of emotions than most humans.

"Yes, I'm fine," Harold said. "Something happened last night." He paused and took a breath, and I felt him standing out on his land looking in my direction, though we were miles apart. "I don't even have the right words for you," he continued. "But I have to ask. Are any of your girls missing?"

"The girls? I don't understand. The woman who works the night shift left at six this morning. She didn't say anything. What's going on over there, Harold?"

"A girl was found out here. I already called the sheriff. Just waiting for him to show up. I thought you should know with the girls and all at the shelter. Don't want to scare you."

"Scare me? What do you mean?"

"The girl's dead. She was killed."

"Killed or murdered, Harold?"

"Terrible thing. Never seen anything like it. It's bad, Hannah. Lord, help me. I never thought I'd live to see something like this happen out here."

"What is it? Just tell me what's going on."

"That poor girl was hacked to pieces. Hannah, there's a monster out there somewhere."

I stopped listening to Harold and started walking back toward the house, where minutes ago my girls were happy and safe. Life turned on a dime. The sooner you learn that in life, the better off you'd be. I grew up watching my mother and father work day and night to keep it all going. That was the best lesson I learned in survival. I bent down to pat Jack standing next to me. My Jack knew there was trouble brewing.

"Harold, are you still there?"

"Did you even hear what I said, Hannah?"

"Yes, I heard you. Now I'm going to speak. No one. No one is going to touch my girls. So help me God, if it's the last breath I take."

CHAPTER THREE

Sheriff Ronnie Hoffman
Edwards County, Texas

"That's one hell of a greeting for a Monday morning, deputy. This better be some Halloween prank."

"No, sir. I got a call from Harold Brune this morning. Might be the missing girl from Del Rio."

I sighed heavily, then took a dog biscuit from a glass jar and deposited it beneath my desk. Butch slept there on a worn Mexican blanket. I watched the deputy for a while, remembering the man had been under my leadership for over twenty years and had never been promoted. I had my reasons.

"Brune said the victim was hacked up pretty good." Deputy Sheriff Tony Stancik reinforced his courage to give the report with a dramatic swig from his forty-eight-ounce can of Atomic Energy. "Said he didn't hear a thing last night. Said it was as bad as it gets, or worse."

I wiped the spittle off my eyeglasses with a handkerchief from my back pocket. I'd worked with Stancik long enough to know the first can of energy drink had taken effect with the result of him spitting his words in all directions of this office.

"Old Man Brune is blind," I said. "Probably some rubber body parts a punk kid threw out there to shake everybody up for Halloween. But the poor fool reported it, so let's take a ride, deputy. Leave the can here. You don't need any more caffeine."

I lifted myself out of the chair and walked into my administrative assistant's office.

"Dolores, we're headed to Brune's place out on 55. Butch is sleeping under the desk. If I'm not back in an hour or so, he may need to go out."

Dolores shook some Red Hots in her mouth from the open box on her desk. While crunching them with her back molars, she made eye contact and nodded.

"I'm driving into San Antonio when I get off," she said, still working on the Red Hots. "Want anything from Costco?"

"Cheeseballs," I said, and slammed the steel-frame door on my way out, while Dolores wrote "cheeseballs" on a green sticky note and added it to her collection of notes on her computer monitor. If anything, Dolores was predictable in her habits.

The drive to Harold Brune's place gave me time to consider my retirement. It was something I did several times a day, creating a little jingle in my head of six more months, five more months, sliding into four more months. I wasn't a lazy man, but I felt I had served my community and done my time. When I took the job, I was an energetic man who believed I was the watch dog for the people of Edwards County. But the years changed, and so did the crimes. I was shorthanded and underfunded in fighting drug trafficking, human trafficking, and the occasional drunks starting fights downtown at the Delta Dawn Bar. It never ended.

I'm getting old, I thought. That human trafficking of the

Mexican girl and the ride into Mexico a few years ago with a cartel on my ass was the first blow. I had worked with a new border agent, a real smart-ass with a chip on his shoulder, but we were able to save a young girl and her family. Hannah did most of the work on that case, but it was the beginning of more traffickers and more victims. I was tired of spinning plates. My body hurt, and I wasn't moving like I used to. But most of all, I hated what was in my head. It made me sick to my stomach how violent this country had become. School shootings. Meth heads blowing up trailers. Human traffickers moving people and drugs on I-10. What the hell happened?

I let the deputy drive. Looking at him behind the wheel, I knew Stancik wasn't a bad lawman. He did the best he could, but the deputy, along with Dolores and local politics, took their toll on my patience, gnawing away a little with each passing year until I was about ate up. I sighed and turned to look at the passing land. Miles and miles of cedar, scrub oaks, and caliche dirt. Maybe I was depressed. No, I knew what was wrong with me. I didn't give a shit anymore; the job had bled me dry.

I could see Harold Brune was having a hard time this morning before I even got out of the truck. The old man was standing on his front porch with a cup of coffee when Stancik pulled into the gravel driveway. He looked anxious, pacing on his porch. You'd think life would finally get a bit easier for an eighty-six-year-old man who served in Vietnam.

A direct descendant of the German immigrants during the Texas Republic, Harold had eked out a living raising goats and leasing land to deer hunters. Leasing land was more lucrative than raising goats, but like most of the old-timers out here, Harold never got used to the hunters' 48-volt hunting carts and fashionable hunting clothes. I'm sure he kept his mouth shut, like most his age, purely out of economics. Social Security wasn't much to live on, so Harold put up with the hunters. The checks never bounced, and the rich hunters from San Antonio, Austin, and Houston tended to leave big tips. So, Harold kept driving his ice cream truck for the hunters. He kept the feeders full, spread the alfalfa, and the bucks came. He rang his bell, and the hunters followed.

It was bad enough knowing someone had been out on his land during the night, but Harold thought there'd been a murder when he was in bed sleeping, surrounded by his dogs. He told Stancik he didn't hear anything through the night. That was odd, considering all the dogs he kept. They hadn't barked? Then he told Stancik about body parts strewn about the property. What was the man's eyesight like? Was he wearing his glasses? Was he even thinking clearly? Getting old was for the birds. Unfortunately, I knew all about that.

When I opened the truck door, he shouted to his dogs, "Go on! Get back on the porch." He slapped his hands together to let the pack know he meant business.

"Good morning, Harold. I understand you found something out on your land." I extended my hand to greet him. I immediately noticed the strength in his grip when our hands met, but he was shaking.

"I'm not sure you're ready for this, sheriff. I'm going to put the dogs in the house, then we'll take a little walk."

I motioned to my deputy to get the yellow crime-scene tape and evidence bags out of the truck. "Don't forget the camera," I added.

As we waited for Harold by the truck, I told my deputy that I wanted to talk to Brune alone. While I was with Brune, I wanted Deputy Stancik to make sure he did a thorough search of the area, looking for evidence like a cigarette butt, footprint, even a possible weapon. I assured the deputy I'd let him know when I needed him, depending on what I learned on my walk with Brune.

The screen door slammed behind Harold, and we walked together about a mile or so from the house, kicking up caliche dust with our boots. For once Stancik listened and followed quietly at a good distance behind us. We walked past an old cement cistern when Harold stopped and pointed to two hands, crudely severed at the wrists, lying beneath a mesquite bush.

An involuntary rush of air escaped from my lips, producing a low whistling sound. Stancik ran toward us screaming, "Oh, God!" and began frantically waving at the swarm of flies circling the severed hands. He stumbled a few feet then vomited on his boots.

Within a few more yards of the mesquite bush were two feet with their soles removed, crudely severed at the shinbones from the legs. Harold was right. The victim had been hacked to pieces.

The old man touched my arm then pointed to the fence in the distance. The head of a young woman was centered on the post. Her eyes were gone. There wasn't a single drop of blood or bloodstain anywhere. It was as though she'd been drained dry before her head was placed on the post.

Stancik continued retching behind us, the evidence kit and tape discarded on the ground with the camera still dangling around his neck. I looked at Brune then walked closer to the fence post.

All the while I kept thinking about the intel I read last week. A drug cartel was suspected of operating near the border outside Del Rio. This cartel was known for using a twisted version of the Palo Mayombe ritual on victims. Dismemberment was their trademark.

I walked back to where Brune and Stancik were standing

together, staring at the detached hands and feet of the woman. She was probably the missing person reported from Del Rio. I knew then my few months to retirement was shot all to hell. It was just a matter of bad luck and death near the border. Yes, sir, as they said, it was all about location, location, location.

"Harold, we're gonna get the remains off your property. Seal off the area. You'll need to keep the dogs tied up till we do. I'll do my best here to get this cleaned up as quick as possible."

The two men shook hands and locked eyes.

"Sheriff, it's a terrible shame what people can do to one another. I saw things like this in Vietnam, but I never thought it would be in my own backyard. No, sir. Can't stop thinking about that poor girl's family."

Stancik and I watched the old man with his head bent down, walking back in the direction of his house. With every step he took, he appeared a bit smaller and more hunched over. I felt his steps reverberate in my chest and throat. I had to agree with the old man; it was a very different world we lived in today.

"Deputy, get yourself cleaned up. Find the number of that new border agent in town. Think his name is Nocona Ketemoczy."

"The Comanche, or is he Mexican? Can't tell."

"Doesn't matter, deputy. Get the man."

CHAPTER FOUR

Nocona Ketemoczy
Kingburger
North State Street
Rocksprings, Texas

Kingburger was the town's hub. Breakfast, lunch, and dinner were appointed the local grub of Tex-Mex, chicken-fried steak, and hamburgers served in a corrugated tin and wood-paneled dining room. I placed my order at the counter, noticing the sign by the register that refills weren't free. You never would have seen a sign like that when I was growing up. Everything in today's world was ruled by the bottom line.

"Miss, change the Coke to an extra-large. Easy on the ice."

It was then I saw the sheriff motioning me to his table. I was expecting his invitation earlier today or something similar to it when I saw the witch while driving into work this morning. She was predictable to me at this point. Her appearances, like leaning against the entrance to Kingburger, and the sounds of her laughter as I walked past her didn't make my heart jump anymore. It was knowing what would follow that caused my anxiety. But I'd been trained as a Marine, so I kept that in check before sitting in front of the big man in town, Sheriff Ronnie Hoffman.

Just as he immediately sized me up as a mixed breed Indian-Mexican with tats of a spear and knife on my forearms, I noticed his "cheater" glasses from the drugstore and his gut overlapping his belt. He stood up halfway from his seat to greet me, offering his hand for his testosterone-fueled handshake.

"Ketemoczy, thanks for meeting me on short notice."

"It's Nocona," I offered, sitting down.

"I recognize that name. Not sure from where. Maybe that John Wayne movie, *Fort Apache?*

I tried not to roll my eyes.

"I'm Comanche-Mexican, not Apache."

"I see. You from around the area?"

"Grew up in Bandera. Did some time with the Marines before border-agent work."

"Marine," he nodded, then cleaned his sunglasses with a paper napkin on the table. The waitress hadn't been by with our food, so I assumed the napkin was from the last customer.

"Why the meeting, sheriff?"

"Just came in from a small ranch off of 55. Female victim was hacked up. Lab should confirm more about who she was in a couple of days."

Before I could reply, I heard laughter behind the sheriff. It was her, the Witch of Sonora, sitting at the next table. *Play it cool, play it cool. The fat man in front of you will think you've lost your mind.*

"Sounds like a job for the boys in blue," I said, giving the witch as little attention as I possibly could. "It's your home turf, sheriff. You don't need a border agent."

"I think the victim is the missing girl reported from Del Rio.

Got a ritualistic murder scene but no blood. Someone could have done the deed elsewhere and thrown the body parts on an old man's ranch as a warning to an enemy."

I didn't reply but continued holding his gaze with the sole purpose of trying to decide whether or not I wanted to work with him. It would be easy to hand it all to DHS, especially knowing the witch was somehow involved. But that also meant slowing it down and politics running the show.

"I wouldn't say I'm used to nutcases, but being a sheriff in a desolate county so close to the border, well, this job has shown me a thing or two over the years. This girl's murder, it's different. Reminds me of a case from the late eighties. Texas college kid went to Mexico for spring break and ended up murdered outside a ranch in Matamoros. Lots of skulls, cauldrons, yeah, like a witch's cauldron, found at that ranch. Turns out the boy's murder and many others were committed by a drug-trafficking cartel run by Constanzo, originally from Miami by way of Cuba. His mother raised him in the Palo Mayombe tradition, something she also practiced. It's a lot like Santería but darker."

I knew those religions just like I knew the witch. I also knew the sheriff was smarter than he looked. I nodded at him.

"Palo Mayombe has origins in Afro-Caribbean culture like Santería," the sheriff said as he searched the restaurant for the waitress and his food. "Uses animal sacrifice and human bones in rituals, but human sacrifice is where the buck stops for me. I'm thinking this girl was murdered by someone like Constanzo and his gang."

"I remember those stories, sheriff. But the playbook has changed. Today's cartels are stronger. More violent. They make the eighties seem like child's play."

"True."

The waitress arrived with our order.

"Thank you, ma'am," the sheriff said with a smile and pulled his plate a little closer to him.

It was an incredible amount of food even for two men. The sheriff's chicken-fried steak was floating in milk gravy with buttermilk biscuits for sopping up the leftovers. I wondered if he would continue talking or pick up a fork.

"Nocona, I need your help, not the entire border patrol. I like to work with small numbers. The fewer involved, the better."

With his intention known, the sheriff worked on his plate. I took a bite of my cheeseburger while both of us watched the other eat.

"Sheriff, I'll help you, but there's parameters. You're not my boss, and I don't like talkers."

"Figured you were a lone wolf. I'll try not to piss you off, considering you're a former Marine."

"Devil Dog in the green machine, sheriff."

The sheriff laughed out loud and pushed his plate from his stomach.

The waitress came by with the check. "Will that be it, sheriff?"

"Do you have any pie?" I asked.

"Pecan and apple. Hold on a minute."

The waitress turned toward the kitchen and yelled above me, "Danny, we got any of that peach cobbler left? Sir, you'll want some of that cobbler. The peaches are from Fredericksburg."

"Sandy, we got two to three servings left," Danny, the cook and owner, replied from the front counter.

"I'll take the cobbler with ice cream on the side. Is the ice cream Blue Bell?"

"We only serve Blue Bell, Sheriff. What'll you have?" The waitress pointed her pencil at me.

"Same here."

We ate our dessert in silence, with the sheriff using his spoon as a forklift for the ice cream. He pushed his bowl back and sighed happily.

"Lunch is on me, partner." He flipped open his wallet and dropped a twenty and ten on the table.

"I got the tip," I said, throwing another ten on the table.

The sheriff stood up and put on his cowboy hat.

"I'd like to introduce you to a friend of mine. She lives outside of town. Runs the Casa de Katia."

"I'll follow you."

Before I walked out of Kingburger, I scanned the dining room for the witch. She was gone. I followed the sheriff's F-150 out of the parking lot, accepting the cold hard fact a lot more people were going to die than the poor girl hacked to death on an old man's ranch.

CHAPTER FIVE

Nocona Ketemoczy
Casa de Katia
Rocksprings, Texas

I followed the sheriff out of town along U.S. 377 until we reached the gate of the Durand Ranch. I knew who Hannah Durand was. Everyone did. The old widow had saved a girl and her family from a cartel several years ago. Part of that rescue involved killing the perpetrator with a .30-06 rifle at close range. There was more than one bullet hole in that man. That was a fact few could forget in the case. Hannah Durand was a formidable woman. She later opened Casa de Katia as a horse-therapy ranch and temporary housing for female victims of human and sex trafficking.

Driving through the caliche dust, I viewed the 640-acre ranch as modest compared to those built by the flood of *nuevo*-rich Austinites.

Kerr and Edwards counties were full of Austin elites with ranch homes fueled by wind turbines and infinity pools carved out of limestone with jackhammers. Of course, that was all fun and games until the first norther hit, making the huge blades of those wind turbines lifeless, frozen in ice. The arrogance of it all reminded me of a TV commercial from my childhood. It was the classic of Mother Nature versus a product meant to be a close substitute but clearly wasn't. In this case it was margarine. The new margarine being marketed was supposed to be just like the real deal. It was so close to butter; the commercial's jingle was "It's not nice to fool Mother Nature." That's what I thought of those big shots in Austin destroying the Hill Country. Buddy, Mother Nature was gonna take your big plans and break 'em all to hell.

I guess Hannah and her late husband had nothing to prove. Cedar post fencing surrounded their ranch with a small ranch house, probably built in the seventies, at the end of a gravel road. The wood and cast-iron windmill behind the house was still working, pumping water into a concrete cistern with each puff of air from the cloudless sky. When I got out of my truck, I saw the bunkhouse and horse corral for Casa de Katia a dozen or so yards away. A few of the girls were saddling their horses and heading for a ride. A woman was filling a water trough and throwing out bales of hay for the horses. I watched them with a longing. My dad and I used to ride together. When he took me to work with him on Saturday, he made me feel like a man though I was nothing more than a skinny kid who could barely get the saddle on by myself. I might have been shoveling horse shit from the stalls for hours, but I was with my best man. He was teaching me his job.

I followed the sheriff to the front door. Hannah opened it after one knock. She probably was watching us come up the road. There she was, the legendary Hannah Durand, over eighty now but straight backed and open faced like a young girl. She sized me up immediately with a nod of her chin.

She greeted the sheriff with the intimacy of an unspoken pact made in Mexico and on this ranch. Violence, death, and duty had bonded them for life. That was the mode of operation in Edwards County, and just about every county close to the border and I-10. I understood it as a Marine and border agent. You got the job done. Period.

She opened the door wider to let us in. In the corner by the door was a .30-06 rifle. I wondered if it was the same weapon used to kill the perpetrator all those years ago.

"I just put on a fresh pot of coffee," she said, looking at me. "Come on into the kitchen."

She poured two large mugs and set them on top of an oak table. The sheriff and I pulled up our chairs. She poured herself a cup and sat down at the head of the table.

"Can I get you some milk and sugar?" she asked me. "I know the sheriff likes his coffee black."

"No, ma'am," I said, smiling at her.

"Now make yourself at home. Got some homemade sugar cookies in that tin in front of you. Grab yourself a napkin," she said, handing me and the sheriff each a paper napkin.

"Hannah, this is border agent Nocona Ketemoczy. He's working with me on a case. A murdered girl was found on a ranch outside Rocksprings."

She reached for my hand across the table and shook it.

"Nice to meet you, Agent Ketemoczy," she said.

"Call me Nocona, ma'am."

That gave me my second smile. Those blue eyes, sky blue, took me in. There was no doubt she had been a beautiful woman all her life. Most women probably hated her for that, but men, this man, felt that power immediately. Beauty, brains, and heart, the trinity of perfection.

"We believe this is the girl reported missing near Del Rio and somehow ended up in Edwards County. We're going to need your help. Maybe some of your girls in the shelter know something."

"Harold Brune called me this morning. He didn't tell me everything, but I know there's trouble. Regardless of that, I'm not going to let you or the agent interview any of my girls."

"No, ma'am. You do it," the sheriff said. "In your own time, in your own way."

I looked around the kitchen and wondered how long those interviews would take. I could hear the girls laughing outside and the sound of the horses running. Then Hannah got up from the kitchen table and looked directly at me.

"You'd be surprised what an old woman can do, Nocona. It's why I still live out here and run the shelter. I think I may surprise you."

I fought the urge to be shocked at her ability to read my mind. There were no coincidences in this life. There was only action and reaction. I was obviously on a path with the witch and Hannah Durand. Good and evil had been following me all my life. By the time I was thirty, I accepted nothing was random. Nothing. I could either be a victim or on fire watch. I chose fire every damn time.

I gave her my best Marine reply. "Ma'am, most of Central and West Texas knows you and what you did for the Morales family. Your work continues to be admired."

"Excuse my French, Hannah. But, Nocona, you can't bullshit her."

The sheriff chuckled and pushed himself up from the kitchen table. It was in my nature to punch a smart-ass, but I caught myself. I finished my coffee in silence.

"Ever heard of Palo Mayombe, Hannah? It's a religion founded in African-Cuban cultures," Hoffman asked.

"No," she said, looking at me, piecing together my story, recognizing the Comanche in me as she must've turned the words “Nocona Ketemoczy” in her thoughts. “But I know evil when I see and hear it.”

“It’s got a dark side, a dangerous side, this religion,” the sheriff added. “I don’t want to exaggerate anything, but I have to be honest with you. Make sure the girls understand they need to tell you anything they see or hear that’s unusual. It goes without saying, they need to be careful and not wander off alone.”

She looked at me again then turned her gaze to the bunkhouse outside her kitchen window.

“Hannah, we’ll show ourselves out,” the sheriff said, standing up. “Give you a call in a few days.”

“Thank you, sheriff. It was nice meeting you, Nocona,” she said, never turning around to look at me or the sheriff. “I’m sure I’ll see you in a few days.”

The sheriff nodded at me. We left the house, got in our separate trucks, and drove off without another word between us. The sheriff got out after crossing the cattle guard to open the gate. He waved at me then drove through. He was probably going back to town. It was too early in the day to call it quits for myself.

Once I crossed the cattle guard, I got out of the truck and locked the gate behind me. There she was, right behind me, sitting on a cedar fence post. The cataract eyes. The toothless mouth. I wondered then if I should drive back to Hannah’s house to warn her. Then it hit me like a ton of bricks. Hannah probably already knew the Witch of Sonora from the Mercado de las Brujas.

CHAPTER SIX

Hannah Durand
Casa de Katia
Rocksprings, Texas

The sheriff and I had a history, as they say. And now I'd have one with Nocona Ketemoczy. He was an old soul, as old as his great-great-grandfather, Chief Ketemoczy. The Great Spirit lived in Nocona, just as it had in his ancestors. Despite the efforts of the Catholic Church's Indian schools, the Great Spirit was never replaced in Nocona's lineage.

When I looked at him in the kitchen, I could imagine the Comanche boys of the late nineteenth century and early twentieth century sitting at their desks at St. Patrick's in Anadarko, Oklahoma. They were as still as fear can make small boys taken from their families, culture, and home.

There was tremendous pain inside Nocona. The pain of generations. The tears of grandmothers and mothers. But soon Nocona, carrying the weight of all those years, would learn the role he would play in this century. He was on a journey. Like the sheriff and me. Our stories were not over, and they would entwine themselves tightly around us until we knew the reason.

That was faith. You had to dig deep into your conscience, grab the ego that makes us feel we're in control, and let it all go. Love for others was the only way to live in peace. It was the very foundation of Jesus's teachings.

Jesus said to love our neighbor as ourselves, meaning our neighbor as everyone we share this Earth with. People found that hard to do. Impossible for the bloated human ego, but it wasn't impossible for divinity. I'd probably never be a saint, but it sure was a task worth working toward instead of the slippery slope of the human superlatives. It was a fool's errand to set your life goals on being the smartest, prettiest, and richest human. There were millions of stories of the short-sighted, lonely life that route offered.

I saw faith as a lifelong process in developing ourselves into the best we could be. People, by nature, were a mixture of hope and damage, depending on what life threw at them. Faith was the one thing that could change all of it for the better. I truly believed that the most damaged person in the world was worthy of love. If it weren't possible, I never would have started Casa de Katia.

My girls, no matter what they did, deserved to be loved. That was the cure for the hurt and anger they felt. It was that simple yet very hard to accomplish once a person has been stripped of dignity and filled with shame.

Nocona's torment came from battling good and evil within. Ava, who came here a few weeks ago, was confused by the same battle within her. Good and evil. Light and dark. That was the way of this world. You had to fight it. You had to have faith to hope for more. Because without hope, there was nothing. And I mean nothing.

I believed this was my last journey on this Earth, helping Nocona find peace and serving the girls in the bunkhouse. Ava especially needed me, and I was determined to solve the mystery surrounding that girl if it was the last thing I did.

It began when the West Texas Coalition Against Trafficking brought her here. I guessed her age to be eighteen, maybe nineteen at the most. She was half starved and battered from walking from Central Mexico and riding the *La Bestia*, the train migrants took to Juarez before crossing over to the US. They often rode on the spine of the train above the boxcars, clinging to an old life and the hope it would soon be better *el otro lado*.

She made her way into Del Rio and was picked up outside Edwards County by the coalition. She didn't have any papers but said she was promised a good job in Kerrville at a landscaping company. She soon learned there was no connection or safety net on this side of the border. Her coyote and money were gone. It was a very familiar story, if she was telling me the truth.

She was a quiet girl, riding horses in the early morning and choosing to sit by herself at meals. The thing that struck me and the counselors most about her was the enormous tattoo on her forearm of a black cauldron with white Xs and Os. Those letters were like hieroglyphics. I was positive there was a double meaning to them. Inside the cauldron were sticks of equal size. In all my years, I've never seen anything like it.

After the sheriff's visit, I began to understand a bit more about Ava and her tattoo. Maybe the tattoo was related to the Palo Mayombe religion the sheriff spoke about. If it was, I'd have to approach her very slowly and carefully. It was too late for today. Maybe before lunch tomorrow. I'd lead that little paint she'd been riding out to the corral for her. The girls tended to be more relaxed around the horses. The last thing I wanted to do was scare her and have her out on the streets again, searching for a safe place to hide.

I scrambled a few eggs for supper. I just wasn't eating as much as I did when I was younger. That's what getting old was. You didn't eat much, and you sure didn't sleep much, either. What you did do was think and remember.

I sat on the front porch listening to the girls talking and laughing in the bunkhouse. A radio played Tejano music, the sounds of home for many of them. One girl sang along with the radio. I thought of their loneliness, their pain, why they ran from their homes or why someone simply took them.

After all this time and my work here, I still couldn't fathom the slave trade run by the cartels. It was too evil and too pragmatic for the mind to accept. Owning a human being was accepting the fact that human life meant nothing. There was no dignity, no rights for the most vulnerable in the world. The cartels and traffickers viewed themselves as gods, determining who lived in freedom and who existed to serve others. It was an arrogance beyond measure. Slavery, human trafficking. Just different labels for a different generation. It was the very worst of human behavior for those who took human beings and for those on this side of the border who used them for sex and labor.

Twilight and its magic hour came to the porch. It was my favorite time of day, thinking of the animals on the ranch, getting their last drink of water before bedding down. I often imagined the deer looking for the security of an overgrown cedar to sleep under for the night. I decided to walk out to the pasture to make sure all was in order before the sun went down, especially the water pump behind the bunkhouse. Jack tagged along.

The water pump had been giving me fits over the past year. It didn't matter how new the pump was, it just never worked as well as the one Joseph put in for me years ago. I should have never replaced it. Like a fool giving away her money, I just got caught up with the latest ranching gimmicks. I hated to think of the animals going without water, so I'd just have to replace it. Although Halloween was right around the corner, the days were dry, in the high eighties, but I knew winter would come, as it always did.

I took my time walking to the pump, stretching each leg, complete steps of each foot, making sure my hips were opened and aligned. That was my only ailment in my eighties. Arthritis, the doc told me, and I agreed. I've become a human barometer with each cold front or rainstorm pushing through, and the pain always went straight to my right hip.

If I were lucky, I might spy a bobcat or whitetail near the water pump. There was talk in town about eradicating the bobcat out on the ranches. Made me furious. Some ranchers were complaining they were predators, getting after their cattle and livestock. I never had that problem in all the years I've been out here, counting nearly sixty. I had always had good ranch management through adequate fencing of our livestock to keeping a steady eye on them when grazing in open pasture. It wasn't right to destroy an animal due to human negligence. I never liked that kind of thinking.

I stopped to take a breather, wiping the sweat off my forehead with my kerchief. I never got tired of the view, groves of cedar, the red-leafed Spanish oaks, and the turning of the natural grasses as the season made way for the harshness of winter.

It was then I heard the old woman. She might have been calling out my name for some time, but I didn't hear her when I was walking through the land with Jack leading the way.

"Hannah." It was a harsh voice, coming deep within her

throat. At first, I thought it was one of the counselors for Casa de Katia calling after me.

Jack started barking. “Calm down, boy,” I said. “Just the animals getting ready for bed, Jack. Come stand by me.”

Then I called out, “Elizabeth! I’m here by the water pump.”

“Hannah,” the voice said, louder.

I turned toward the direction of the voice, and there stood an old woman not two feet from me. I don’t know how I didn’t hear her approach, but Jack did. He snarled and jumped up at her. The haggard old woman stepped backward and stared at me through her milky eyes. A volatile stench surrounded her and the filthy, tattered dress she wore.

“Who are you? You have no right to be on this land.”

She laughed with a toothless grin, and just as she appeared to me, she was gone, enveloped by the last of the twilight hour into the approaching dark spreading across the October sky. Jack began barking and leaped toward the spot she had disappeared. I stood firm. I knew who she was.

Evil had returned to my home.

CHAPTER SEVEN

Nocona Ketemoczy
Rocksprings, Texas

I lay in my bed staring at the ceiling occasionally lit by lightning flashes, wondering why I was in another shitty apartment complex in the middle of nowhere. I couldn't count the number of times in my life I had done that.

Tonight's thunderstorm came out of the Panhandle. Each change of the season, spring to summer, fall to winter, brought storms of increasing intensity, as if Mother Nature had to prove once again who was really in control. She could have been punishing us for treating our nest like a toilet bowl.

I thought about Hannah, just like I thought about the witch. I felt both of them in the movement of stale air circulated by the ceiling fan. Those lonely hours between three a.m. and the ringing of the alarm were a helter-skelter of women, places, and regrets. I was beginning to regret taking this job and partnering with the sheriff. The urge to get out of this bed and pack a few things was strong. I had lots of practice in calling the boss man and saying, "I quit." The next step was sequential, leave town, maybe even the country. *Nocona, the wanderer, was running away to nowhere one more time.*

When a crack of thunder pounded in my ears, the sweet spot of Rocksprings lost power. No more humming of the ceiling fan or AC. For another hour in bed, I wondered if I should quit or not, when the sweat of my body cooled, and I passed out. I didn't wake up until my cell started ringing at seven. I had slept through my alarm.

"It's your buddy, Nocona. Stop burning daylight," the sheriff said. "Got another body. A young girl found out on Highway 377. Looks to be the same ritualistic murder scene. Time to *vámanos*."

"Sheriff," I said, still half asleep and my body damp with night sweats. "Sooner or later, I'm going to either quit my job or let my boss know what I'm doing."

"Nocona, I know your boss. He's busy filling out forms for the feds. Continue status quo with your designated rounds, then get out here. You'll see my truck."

"Yeah, right." I said and hung up. I stumbled to the toilet and got a hot shower, thanks to Pedernales Electric Co-op returning power after the storm.

I did my status quo as a border agent, stopping by the station then driving in the dust of the endless dirt roads to deploy remotely monitored seismic sensors. Everywhere I went I could see signs of migrant crossings: empty water bottles, food wrappers, and used diapers.

My job as an agent was nothing more than a dog chasing its tail. As long as Mexico, Haiti, and all the failed governments of the world continued to let the thugs run the show, people would come pouring across. When people were homeless and running in fear, criminals were on the make for new opportunities and ways to make money. The more vulnerable, the easier the pickings were. The cartels had a field day with the chaos—the inmates really had the keys this time.

I contacted the border agent station in Del Rio about the scene there, hoping to glean information about the murders in Edwards County. Josie McKenney was an agent I'd been working with on and off over the past year. A tough chick who served as an Army Ranger in Afghanistan, she was one of the few in the agency I trusted. It could have been her time in Afghanistan. We were alike in some ways. She moved around a lot and didn't bore you with the reasons why.

"How's Del Rio treating you, Jo?"

"A lot like you, surveying the goat trails. Some weird shit showed up a few weeks ago though."

"Same here. Soup sandwich. Your classic ritualistic crime scene."

"Roger. I started surveillance on an old ranch house with acreage near the Rio Grande and Canyon Rim, close to Seminole Canyon State Park. Lot of movement. Even located an airstrip. Wonder what it's used for, right?"

"What's your boss think?"

"Noco, you know me better than that." She laughed. The woman had the best damn laugh in the world. "He knows what little I tell him, but I've kept my mouth shut about the airstrip until I can get out there and have a look around."

"Jo, I got to meet someone, but I want to continue this conversation. Let me take you to lunch this Saturday at Molcajetes on Veterans. On me, of course."

"Are you asking me out on a date, Noco?" She laughed a long time on that one, but I could almost hear her questioning my motives behind that laughter.

"Sure. I like to mix business with pleasure."

"You're such a tease, Noco. Save it for the other girls," she said. "Look, I'll meet you on Saturday, but I'm coming hungry since it's on you. Change that to hungry and very thirsty."

I was about to say something clever, but before the thought came, she said, "Got to go, Romeo. I'm still on the clock, and my cell is blowing up with texts."

CHAPTER EIGHT

Nocona Ketemoczy
U.S. 377, north to Junction

When I got to the crime scene, Deputy Sheriff Stancik was puking behind the sheriff's truck. No doubt the man had a weak gut. Hoffman was taping off the crime scene until he heard my truck. He waved me on over with black plastic gloves covering his hands.

"The only thing different about this scene compared to the one at Brune's place is the victim's head is missing," the sheriff said, wiping his forehead free of sweat with the back of his sleeve. "But I don't like to share evidence, knowing your doubts about being here. Are you playing on the team or not?"

"Just doing what needs to be done, sheriff. The boss knows I'm looking into the first missing girl from Del Rio. That's a border issue, possibly trafficking. There's not much more than that. I'm here this morning. That's the biggest commitment I can give you right now."

"Just another noncommittal male," the sheriff laughed. Hoffman was a real jokester, at least in his own mind.

I left the sheriff to his sense of humor as he picked up body parts and placed them in evidence bags. I walked the area looking for bloodstains, boot tracks, anything to help build our case. Nothing. It was clean except for a plastic grocery bag clinging to a clump of bittercress stalks near the shoulder of the road.

I opened up the bag and found a paper receipt dated from yesterday. Someone had purchased a twelve-pack of Natty Ice, a pack of Marlboro Reds, and a bag of pork rinds from the H-E-B on Pecan Street over in Del Rio. It was paid for with a credit card.

"Sheriff," I said, holding up the thin piece of paper. "We got our first lead."

"Good. Time is ticking away for the next victim and me. The locals won't stop calling, reminding me of my age, thinking I'm too damn old to handle this case."

"I'm headed to Del Rio tomorrow to talk to an agent. I'll stop by the H-E-B and get a trace on this receipt."

"I'm not sitting on my ass for twenty-four hours with a freak out there decapitating women. Give me the receipt. I'll go to Del Rio now."

"Not your jurisdiction, man. There's intel from the Del Rio agent. She's connecting missing girls to a location outside of town. They may have been used as drug mules. You connect with Hannah."

"I'd like to remind you of a prior conversation we had, Noco. Not that long ago. At the Kingburger over a chicken-fried steak. We're partners here, buddy. Our goal is to get the freak off the street as soon as possible."

"Don't bow up on me, sheriff. It's a waste of time for both of us."

The sheriff looked down at his boots covered in dust. He knelt down, took his night club from its holster, and drew a few lines in the sand. I knew what he was thinking. He was thinking about retirement, how damn hot it was, and me, the Mexican-Comanche standing in front of him.

"It doesn't have to be this hard, sheriff," I offered. "Let me do my job, and you do yours. Call me if you learn something. You're better with Hannah than I am. I get the creeps around her and that ranch."

The sheriff stood up and looked me square in the eyes, offering his hand. I don't know if the Old West handshake and eye contact was out of habit or if he agreed with what I said.

"I'll let you know what happens in Del Rio," I said and shook his hand out of respect.

"Stancik! I'm going to take your man card from you," the sheriff shouted at the deputy. "Wrap it up before the local ladies head out for lunch."

Still holding steady to the tailgate of the sheriff's truck, Stancik walked over and grabbed a paper towel out of the truck cab and wiped his mouth clean.

"I'm trying my best, sheriff. The smell and the flies are getting to me," he said before bending over and puking on his boots.

Hoffman sighed heavily then looked at me one more time. I took it as permission to leave, so I drove back to Rocksprings. I was behind on paperwork. Submitting reports ate up my time when I needed to be out in the field. But you got to feed the machine when you're working for the feds.

As I passed the Visitor Center, I saw the old witch sitting with her legs crossed on a repurposed church bench out front. The irony almost made me laugh. She began pointing to a flyer posted on the center's front door advertising tours of the Devil's Sinkhole, the cave outside of town that descends more than 150 feet in one fatal drop. Of course, the witch would love the Devil's Sinkhole. No telling how many bones were piled on top of each other at the bottom of that pit. Cowboys. Indians. Settlers. Outlaws. Missing girls. They were all there as testimony to the violence through the ages.

The mindset of people touring places like that was of the same depravity as people taking pictures in front of Robb Elementary School in Uvalde. Just sixty-eight miles from Rocksprings, it was another little town that made world news with a school shooting.

Twenty-one died that day, blown away by a former student. But the real gut punch was the video of the motionless cops in the school hallway listening to the screams of the dying children and the rally of shots being fired by the crazed gunman. The cops waited and listened because they were too damn afraid to move.

But what rolled in my mind over and over was the unforgettable video clip of a cop using the hand-sanitizer dispenser out in the hallway, the same hall that led to the classroom where children were being gunned down. An hour and seventeen minutes passed with cops standing frozen. An hour and seventeen minutes passed before some of my brothers with the U.S. Border Patrol Tactical Unit engaged the shooter.

The Witch of Sonora fed on fear, chaos, and violence. I often imagined she visited the graveyard where those Robb Elementary School kids were buried, laughing at the cowardice of the human race.

I spent the rest of the day writing reports and returning emails while fighting the urge to buy whiskey and drink myself to sleep back at the apartment. But I knew that scenario. I wouldn't sleep on whiskey. I'd only toss and turn all night, thinking, remembering Afghanistan, and talking to the witch sitting in the recliner next to the TV.

I walked out of the office at six p.m. and picked up a frozen pizza and a six-pack for supper. To get my stamina up after the gut bomb, I threw knives at a target I put on the back of the bathroom door.

My dad got me into knife throwing when I was twelve. The Comanche held knife-throwing contests when my dad was a kid. It was something of pride to be able to concentrate on a target and throw a knife with precision. To be the best of the best among the Comanche with a knife, that was a thing during my dad's time. The Flying Blades, a local knife club, met once a week at Delta Dawn's. I'd been invited, but I wasn't a joiner.

I had all the knives my dad gave me through the years. My favorite was the Smith & Wesson Bullseye he got me for my twelfth birthday. I threw it at the target's center until sweat poured down my arm onto the floor. That level of concentration always cleared my head.

Tired, I lay on the bed, thinking of Del Rio and Jo. With the hypnotic ceiling fan above, I mapped out what I wanted from tomorrow. A clear direction in this case and a chance to know her better would be ideal. I smiled thinking of her.

When I thought of her in Afghanistan, one beautiful image remains from all the horror: Jo pulling her mass of red hair to her shoulder and braiding it with her fingers, then tying it off with a rubber band she kept around her wrist. At the same time, she was delivering intel in a measured voice of confidence. She was a hell of a woman. Plus, that laugh of hers was like the bow on a perfect package. That image and sound cured me many long nights when I hated myself and the world around me.

CHAPTER NINE

Nocona Ketemoczy
H-E-B, Pecan Street
Del Rio, Texas

The 8 a.m. scene at the H-E-B in Del Rio was no different than any other grocery store across America. The pharmacy near the entrance doors had a line of people waiting for refills, while eager shoppers took advantage of reduced prices on produce and meat nearing their expiration dates.

I asked for the store manager at the customer service counter. While Mark Garza was being paged, I admired the balancing act of a clerk working on a display of Ranch Water. It was the soup du jour of the calorie-counting beer drinker. H-E-B was marketing its own jalapeño-flavored version. I decided to pick up a six-pack for Jo when the manager approached me.

"Is there a problem, sir? How can I be of service?"

While showing him my badge, I asked, "Do you have an office where we can talk in private?"

He nodded and ushered me to a dimly lit hallway lined

with shopping carts of dented canned goods, expired bread and doughnuts, and a mop bucket full of dirty water. He unlocked his office door and sat behind a metal desk cluttered with framed pictures of children, employment applications, and an e-cigarette he began sucking on.

"Have a seat. Just throw those paper towels on the floor."

"Thank you, Mr. Garza," I said and placed the paper receipt directly in front of him. "I'm investigating a homicide in Edwards County that may have ties to Del Rio. I found this receipt from your store. Can you provide me with more information about the person who purchased these items and paid for them with a credit card?"

"Not sure I can do that," he said, looking down at the receipt. "But I'll give it a try."

He grabbed a notepad off his desk, took a few notes, and gave me back the receipt.

"Wait here. I'll be back in a few." Garza left with his e-cigarette and notepad in hand.

Killing time, I picked up the picture frames on his desk. He must have been a kid when he married, his four kids posing with his pretty wife ranged in age from upper elementary to high school. Garza looked to be in his early forties. He probably started the job in high school, stocking until he made his way up to manager. You had to admire him for that.

I couldn't find fault with a man who was a father, working every day to feed his family. It wasn't my story, probably never would be. I never met a woman interested enough in a future with me, much less carrying our child.

My mind wandered to Jo. I never heard her talk of marriage and kids the times we were working together or out on the town as friends. The woman had so many layers. She'd only let you see what she wanted you to see. Maybe she didn't need a man or kids. Maybe she did. Maybe one day she'd peel back some of those layers for me.

Garza came back and handed me a new piece of paper from his notepad with a name written at the top. "I got a name for you. Lee Chapman."

"Thank you. I got it from here," I said. Motioning toward the picture frames on his desk, I added, "Nice family you have there."

"They're the reason I get up every morning," Garza said. "Keep the streets and schools safe for them out there, agent. Once you find Lee Chapman, bury him six feet under the county jail."

"Thank you for your time, sir."

I had two hours before meeting Jo, so I made a few phone calls, one to the office to run a check on the name and one to Sheriff Hoffman.

"Got a name for you, Hoffman. Lee Chapman. Already called it in to Customs and Border Protection."

"Damn it to hell, Nocona. I thought we had an agreement to work this case together, without other agencies slowing the process down."

"We are. I occasionally have to play with the people who give me a paycheck."

"Check. When you coming back?"

"I'll stop by tomorrow. Got some personal business to take care of."

"In Del Rio? That's right. The agent you're seeing is a woman."

"Nunya, Ronnie. Got that. None of your business, man."

"You're so transparent, Nocona. You're seeing a woman. Good to know you're somewhat human." The sheriff started laughing then hung up.

The sheriff, who also lauded himself as a comedian, needed

a second job on *The Tonight Show*. The thought of that gave me a headache as the hot morning sun beat down into the truck cab.

It was another scorcher with temps in the high eighties. I had sweat through my uniform shirt, and it was only half past ten. I had enough time to go buy a shirt before meeting Jo for lunch. I couldn't remember the last time I made the effort to buy a new shirt to meet a woman, much less worry about sweat in my armpits.

I was setting myself up hard with these thoughts. There were more negatives than positives in losing my head over Jo. I could completely blow this case and get fired. Jo and I were colleagues. I needed her intel on the ranch outside town. Nothing more. I couldn't allow sex, much less love, to ruin our friendship and work. I was too old to keep making that stupid mistake, but women were a very hard habit to break.

When I walked into the restaurant wearing my new shirt, a black button-up with prickly pears in deep green, I felt like a schoolboy. Nervous and excited. I still hadn't let the middle-age gut have its run, so I made the effort to tuck in my shirt when I saw her from across the room. Jo's big green eyes and sexy mass of hair sent adrenalin rushing through my veins like a brush fire.

She was laughing, waving me over. It made me think she liked my shirt. I stood in front of her, then placed the plastic bag of Ranch Water under the table. She got up from her chair and hugged me.

"Cool shirt, Noco. Love the prickly pears," she said, smiling. "Did you buy it to impress me?"

"Yes, ma'am."

"Such a polite young man," she said, laughing.

CHAPTER TEN

Hannah Durand
Casa de Katia
Rocksprings, Texas

I dressed that morning to pull weeds out of the vegetable garden before it got too hot. I had one of August's old shirts on to protect my skin from the sun and bugs. The collard greens were already coming in good, so I set some aside for myself and the girls. Collards with bacon, onion, and cornbread were a full meal for me. You don't move around as much when you're old; you just don't need all that food.

With thistle weeds in my gloved hands, I looked up from my work and saw Ava riding that feisty sorrel, Clara. The horse's mane of red and gold mingled with the black silk rope of Ava's hair as she placed her head close to Clara's neck. Ava appeared to be a pretty good rider and had obviously spent some time on a horse during her young life. Besides, Clara wasn't the type of horse to tolerate an amateur. Her typical behavior with a novice was to throw the unsuspecting rider off as soon as she could. Her other shenanigans included breaking out in a hard run and bucking this way and that until the rider hit the ground.

I watched as they rode as one, and it reminded me of coming to this ranch as a young bride. I brought two suitcases, my grandmother's accordion, a horse trailer, and my horse, Flame. Flame was my first love. She was an intelligent girl, hardy and strong muscled. I loved her, and she loved me. Her gentle disposition helped me through the emotional days of my teenage years, as well as my insecurity as a young bride married to an older man. Flame gave me many happy days and evenings out here on the ranch. We'd often ride with August and Hawk, his Morgan. That breed could trace its lineage back to a stallion from the late 1700s. Hawk was a beautiful animal with a solid black coat. Probably the most versatile horse we ever owned. He was good on the trail and moving the cattle, especially during a violent storm. Our son learned to ride his first horse with Hawk. He was a hard worker and good natured.

To know the love of a good man and the friendship of a beautiful animal were gifts unmeasurable to me. They gave me the happiest years of my life as we rode together on this timeless land through creek beds, open prairies, and cedar thickets.

I left the weeds in a plastic bucket I kept near the garden and whistled for Jack and June to join me at the corral. June looked up at me but wasn't budging. She was a lazy girl, lounging around with that fat cat, Rusty Bucket. Jack stretched in the midmorning sun and ran toward me, happy for a rub behind the ears. I walked to the corral with him leading the way, like he always did.

My intention was to talk to Ava without upsetting her. I waved her over to the gate. She pretended not to see me and gave Clara a good run in a wide circle around the breadth of the corral. Well, I was good at the game of patience. So, I stood with Jack and watched the horse and the girl as one in a cloud of dust. When she finally stopped, I called her.

"Ava, let's get Clara some water after that ride."

She looked up, but she didn't smile. Jack and I walked over to them. When I stood in front of her without a word, she finally dismounted.

Ava wasn't shy. No, ma'am. This gal refused to look at me because she wasn't engaging. Period. This was the same Ava everyone came to know since she got here. I knew she didn't eat or mix with the other girls in the bunkhouse. Ava kept to herself. From the few conversations Elizabeth had with her, Elizabeth said her English was as good as hers. So, there was no language problem. This was all about Ava hiding her past and the future she was planning when she got out of here.

Bits and pieces of young lives were all we usually heard out here. Who knew if the girls were telling me the truth or telling me what they thought I wanted to hear. On this side of the border, they could easily rewrite their histories and become whomever they wanted to be. But I knew better. I knew people could never really run from their past.

My mind was still so tangled by the recent murders and the strange tattoo on Ava's forearm that I didn't know if I was coming or going. But one thing was for sure, Ava knew more than she was letting on. I hoped to change that.

When the sheriff explained Palo Mayombe, I knew enough to be concerned for all the girls. Later that evening I Googled it. Ronnie was right. It was a mixture of several religions: spiritism, Roman Catholicism, and an African-Cuban belief. The captured people of Africa sold into slavery brought some of these beliefs to the sugarcane plantations of Cuba.

The Palo Mayombe followers worshipped a spirit they believed held power over the living and the dead. At the center of their religious ceremonies was a black cauldron. The same cauldrons we often associated with Halloween and witches.

At the command of its owner, the cauldron of evil spirits would do his bidding. I thought of voodoo dolls and how the owner of the doll inflicted pain on victims with a needle inserted into different parts of the doll. Control and power were the game. The same game that's played all over the world, again and again. Someone or something wanted to play that game on my land.

After hours of searching, I came across a website with a photograph of the cauldron and the Palo Mayombe worshippers standing around it. My heart just about jumped out of my chest when I saw the cauldron filled with sticks and human bones that matched Ava's tattoo down to every horrifying detail.

I scared myself to death that night, thinking of Ava's tattoo and the old hag visiting me here. Jack knew her intention was evil. Those cataract eyes of hers, the mocking voice teasing me. I prayed the Rosary in bed that night, over and over. And I knew with every spoken word of "Hail Mary, full of grace, the Lord is with thee," there were millions of people around the world who thought my faith, my religion were evil superstitions created to control people.

Now, here I was after reading all the things on the internet, looking at Ava standing next to Clara. It should have been the most innocent sight of a young girl with a beautiful horse. But it wasn't. Perception and reality were two very different things, especially in today's world. My eyes were focused on her every move as she took Clara's reins and tied them to a post.

"Clara's one of my favorites," I said, watching her eyes take me in, measuring my strength, perhaps even my vulnerability as an old woman. "I'm glad you're enjoying her."

Ava stroked the horse's neck and nodded without so much as a word out of respect.

"Let's walk back to the stable together," I said. "We'll get Clara some water and let her rest." Ava nodded and led Clara to the water trough without a word.

"I haven't had a chance to visit with you, Ava. I'd like to invite you to the house once Clara is settled. I made some banana bread with pecans last night. I thought you might like some."

She followed Jack and me a few paces back to the house. Choosing not to walk alongside us was another example of her not trusting me. But once I got on the porch and opened the front door wide for her, she did follow me into the house. She was still walking as slow as Christmas, but I knew why. She was delaying the conversation she knew we would have in the kitchen. I suspected her story was far darker than someone who was cheated by a coyote with false promises of a good-paying job.

With her arms folded across her chest, she sat quietly at the kitchen table. She wouldn't look at me or talk to me. Instead, she began chewing the nail on her thumb. I gave her a glass of milk and a slice of banana bread. Ava knew. And I should have been more aware that she wouldn't be fooled by a tea party with an old lady. She lived on the streets too long. The game of give-and-take was how she survived out there. She learned early in life that free didn't mean free when someone offered you something. You had to give in return, and the cost might be far more than expected.

"Ava, I can tell you're very unhappy this morning. Have I made you feel uncomfortable?"

"No."

"I see. I'm afraid you may be upset with the recent news of the murder committed not far from here. I asked Elizabeth to let all of you know what was going on, so we could help you if it triggered anything. I know you've had a difficult time since you left your home."

"I miss my family. I've made some terrible mistakes," she replied with her head down.

"Then please let me help you."

"I don't know who to trust. I can't even trust myself."

"You can trust me, Ava. My only intention is to help the girls here. It's my life's work." I sat next to her and placed my hands over her forearm. "Tell me how I can help. You don't have to be afraid. No matter what you tell me, I won't judge you. I won't make you leave. This is your home until you say otherwise."

Soon, her tears fell on the slice of untouched banana bread in front of her. I squeezed her hand softly, and she began sobbing. Her thin shoulders shook with emotion, and she cried with the intensity of what she had endured alone.

Through all her pain and suffering, I would not let go of her hand. We stayed like that, hand in hand, both crying, until Ava spoke.

She hid her face in her hair, so I couldn't see her. "*Señora, he hecho algunas cosas malas.*"

"What happened to you out there? You can trust me, Ava."

"*Obeah. Muy mal.*"

"Help me understand. My Spanish is terrible, so please take your time. Drink a little of this milk, Ava, and breathe in and out slowly. We have all day and night if we need it."

"Evil things. Evil, terrible things." Ava rubbed her tattoo. "I did things, horrible things, *señora*, that can't be forgiven. By God or anyone else."

She was choking on every syllable, then stopped to drink the glass of milk in front of her.

"Ava," I said, taking her face in my hands. "It will be okay. Don't be afraid here. Tell me so I know how to help you."

"*Muy mal*, I was a drug mule, carrying drugs on my back, like a stupid donkey. Sometimes those drugs were pushed deep inside me. No baby will ever grow in my belly. No man will ever want me. There's no escaping, *señora*, for what I've done. *Me escapé, pero él me encontrará*. I must leave, or he will find me and kill me. I know too much."

I took her in my arms and held her tightly until she stopped crying. Later, after she calmed down, we walked back to the bunkhouse together, her head heavy and low on my shoulder. I felt I was carrying her, with every joint in my body searing with pain every inch of the way. Once inside the bunkhouse, I walked slowly to her bed. I took her boots off, pushed aside the bedspread and sheets, and tucked Ava into bed.

I sat on the edge of her bed and placed a wet washcloth across her forehead to soothe her, then washed the line of dirt and sweat from around her neck. Each time I touched her face and neck with the damp cloth, I reminded her I was a friend, and that I would help her.

She opened her eyes once I removed the washcloth from her face and said, "*Muy mal*. He did this." She touched the tattoo on her forearm.

"Who?" I pleaded. "Who did this to you?"

"Lee."

"Who?" I didn't understand.

"Lee Chapman."

"We'll never let him hurt you again, Ava. *Nunca*."

"He keeps a cauldron and spirits. They give him powers. No one can stop him. You cannot kill him or the power he has."

"Like the cauldron in your tattoo?"

The lights in the bunkhouse began flickering, and Ava trembled.

"He's here with the evil spirits. You cannot stop him," Ava cried.

"Ava, listen to me. The lights are flickering because of shoddy electrical work done when I built the bunkhouse. Nothing more. We get a little wind out here, and the lights flicker sometimes. There is no evil power over us. *Nunca*. Lee Chapman is not a god. He is a monster, and his time on this Earth is numbered. I'll see to that."

She began to cry again, weeping from the pains of the past with dread for the future. She felt trapped, no matter which way she turned; nothing offered hope. I imagine there were a lot of broken people who hated getting out of bed each morning, knowing that another day on this Earth was just not worth the heartache and effort.

I sat with her until her eyes closed and her breathing steadied. I turned out the lights and closed the door behind me.

Elizabeth was in the shelter office doing paperwork when I came out of the bunkhouse. She was still a stunning woman with black hair streaked with gray, scuffed ropers, and tight jeans worn like sausage casing.

"You've been in the bunkhouse," she said, reading my face. "Something going on?"

"Just talking to Ava. I heard a little more of her story."

"Is she pregnant? How far along is she?"

"What would make you think that, Liz?"

"I was pregnant and unwed about her age. I recognize the same pain and confusion."

Remembering that time too well, I gave her a sympathetic smile. Joseph had broken my heart when he told me he was an idiot for getting Elizabeth pregnant. In the end, despite the lack of help, never once did he shirk his duties and responsibilities to the baby or to Elizabeth. She didn't talk much during those hard days.

"A pregnancy would have shown up in the initial health check, wouldn't it?" I asked.

"I suppose."

"She did tell me about a man in her past."

"There are a million stories out there of girls getting used by bad men. Nothing worse than being young and naïve."

"She's terrified of him. He treated her horribly. Well, you know the stories out here, Elizabeth. We've heard so many of them."

"Poor Ava. He's probably the man that got her into trafficking."

"We'll need to set up a private session with the psychologist when she comes out again," I said, turning to go. "Will you schedule it?"

"Of course, Hannah."

I nodded at Elizabeth, left her to do her paperwork, and then walked back to the house with Jack. I spotted my first monarch butterfly of the season, resting on the milkweed plants near the front porch. Year after year I looked for them in October, when they began their migration path from Canada to Mexico. So vulnerable with their tiny wings, flying thousands of miles to escape the dark of another Canadian winter.

"Jack, let's sit on the porch," I said, emotionally drained from my talk with Ava. "Let's sit and enjoy our new guest a bit. Soon, there'll be a lot more to watch."

I pulled my straw hat off and hung it on the back of August's old rocking chair. Jack rested on the doormat where the girls had left their carved pumpkins earlier.

I watched with Jack as the monarch fed on a milkweed

plant near the porch. The brilliant orange-red wings of the butterfly floated delicately above the milkweed before flying over to land, for just a moment, on Jack's nose. The more Jack barked, the more I laughed until the weight of the butterfly's wings took my unsettling thoughts to a place of peace.

CHAPTER ELEVEN

Nocona Ketemoczy
Molcajetes Restaurant
Del Rio, Texas

"I see you didn't wait on me to start drinking," I laughed, sitting down directly in front of Jo, not wanting to miss a single thing she said or did.

"That's right, Noco. I started a tab in your name." She licked the salt off the rim of her margarita. "Don't pout. I'm only one up on you."

I picked up the menu so I could hide and regroup. The perfume she was wearing left me fumbling. I'd never known her to wear perfume, much less a dress. But there she was across from me, smiling, in that incredible dress with silver earrings caressing her bare shoulders.

"I'm having the street tacos with brisket. Corn tortillas," I said.

"I was just thinking about the last time we shared a meal.

Our unit was on patrol at a village outside of Kabul. There was an exchange of fire, and we were tying up loose ends. We came up on some goats wandering around. You asked when was the last time we had cabrito. Before we could answer, you took a goat kid, slit its throat, and put it on a makeshift barbecue pit. The only thing missing from that meal was the tortillas and jalapeños. I was impressed! You've always been the man who made things happen, no matter the circumstances," she laughed.

I smiled at her, giving her the green light to be completely in charge. I remembered the goat and smiles that meal gave us on a typical rough day in the field. But I didn't deserve Jo's compliment. She was the take-charge woman in Afghanistan. On reconnaissance, she'd always delivered intel with her left hand on her left hip. It was a sexy stance but unintentional on her part. That was how the woman moved, unaware of the effect her body had on men. She was a soldier and one hundred percent into being a damn good one. There was no false girly-girl, winking away her sexuality to get a charge out of a guy. She'd never stoop that low. There was no pretense or game playing. She felt equal to a man. Because she was.

"Go ahead and order for us," I said, "if you know what you're having."

She waved the waiter over.

"Two more margaritas," she told the waiter, and to me she added, "There's no Don Juan here, Noco. You'll have to make do with Patrón."

"Do you want your drinks before the meal, ma'am?" the waiter asked.

"You can bring everything at once. Bring me the enchilada platter. I'd like mine with red gravy. My date will have the street tacos with brisket. Corn tortillas. Onions and cilantro on the side, please. We'll take a large guac. We'll share it, Noco. Need more hot sauce and chips. Thank you very much."

Once the waiter was gone, she pulled her chair closer to the table and looked directly at me.

"Noco, we can have a little fun with business. No need to have that look of panic on your face. I promise to quit torturing you once the food arrives."

Her laughter filled the restaurant, and a few patrons turned to see what the noise was all about.

"Jo, absolutely, but the bodies of little girls are lining up, and I don't have a clear direction in any of it. Did you go back out to Canyon Rim?"

"Yeah, even checked out the area around Amistad Reservoir Loop. New items at Canyon Rim near the airstrip," she said then stopped to finish her margarita. "There's two shipping containers out there I didn't see before."

"I wonder what that's all about. Stockpiling weapons? Ammunition? Drugs?"

"You know what those are for, Noco? The cocaine trade from Colombia to Amsterdam is good at repurposing shipping containers into soundless torture chambers, complete with pliers, blowtorches, and a dentist's chair with shackles. Our homeowner over in Canyon Rim gets an A for copycatting."

"Did you get into the shipping containers?"

"No, I didn't have the right tools on me. I did get into one of the outdoor buildings. There was a wall of shelves lined with human skulls and some other freaky medieval crap. Like black cauldrons with bones and bird talons in them. Bones could've been animal or human. Sent a few to the lab. We'll see what happens there."

The waiter returned with our margaritas first. I guess the kitchen was having a hard time getting the orders out. The place was packed. We drank in silence, thinking about the real work ahead in this case. The bones were probably human, and we'd soon be facing the nut job who put those bones in a cauldron. When the food came, Jo sighed and looked at me.

"Can we have fun now?"

"Yeah, but you shouldn't go out there alone. Too risky."

"I'm a grown-ass woman, Noco," Jo said with a smile. "Sounds like you're getting a little touchy-feely in your old age."

The waiter brought our food. I took the opportunity to toast the very good idea of taking a break and enjoying the company.

"*Salud*. To feeling and not thinking."

She laughed and clinked her glass against mine. "*Salud*."

The mistake in drinking a few margaritas with a good friend was drinking a few more margaritas with a good friend. Despite all my planning and hard lessons from the past, I stopped thinking completely and fell hard for her. I followed her Jeep out of the restaurant parking lot back to her place, a vintage bungalow of white stucco in south Del Rio.

Jo drove into the single-car driveway in front of the house. I parked on the street, noticing the charm of the place with its arched window casings in the front. There wasn't much grass in the yard, but that was the norm out here. Green lawns were for the mega rich. A lone cedar tree covered the side patio. Jo had a few potted plants and cacti out there near a low-hung hammock just above the faded Saltillo tile. It was a sweet spot for a house. I was happy for her and felt encouraged to ditch the shit box I inhabited in Rocksprings.

We stood together on the covered porch near the front door. When she bent her head down to unlock it, I kissed the side of her neck. She laughed and pulled away from me to open the front door.

We entered a living room of hardwood floors and a barrel-vaulted ceiling. She flipped the lights on.

“How do you like my house, Noco? It’s a rental, but it’s got a whole new feel for me. I’ve spent too many years living in an apartment, awakened by my neighbor flushing the toilet next door. I got a little space now.”

“Happy for you, Jo. It’s a sweet place,” I said, wrapping my arms around her waist and smelling the vanilla-scented shampoo in her thick red hair.

“You want a glass of water? I need to hydrate after the margaritas,” she said, pulling away from me.

“Water is for quitters. Been a long time since I’ve relaxed, Jo.” I said, trying to keep things light. I knew she was nervous. I was too.

She laughed and walked into the arched doorway of the kitchen. She drank a glass of tap water near the sink and stayed there, quietly thinking. We were probably thinking the same thing.

The next step could go either way for us, but was it worth the risk to our friendship? My spotty past with women was not a good indicator, so I had no false hope things would be different this time around. Regardless, I wanted to keep this amazing woman in my life.

As if she’d read my thoughts, Jo turned around and took my hand. She led me into her bedroom in the back of the house. I sat on the edge of the bed covered in a white chenille cotton spread and watched her move toward the two windows on the west side of the room, where outside a bougainvillea spread its hot pink blooms across a wrought-iron railing. She closed the bamboo shades against the white heat of the October sun.

When she turned toward me, the filtered light from the

bamboo shades played across her face and body. Her smile was shy and her movement hesitant when she walked away from the window and toward the bed.

I stood up and kissed her with my heart exploding in my chest.

CHAPTER TWELVE

Sheriff Hoffman
Edwards County, Texas

Who the hell was Lee Chapman? Let me list the many hats the monster wore. He worked for La Nueva Familia Michoacana smuggling fentanyl into the US for the past few years. In the past six years, a quarter of a million or so Americans died from fentanyl overdoses. The likes of Lee Chapman were poisoning us. It was a sure bet to say we lost the war on drugs. "Epidemic" was the word the feds used now in sound bites on drug trafficking and addiction.

You see, when there was a drug war, it was law enforcement against the dope pushers. We were vigilant in the fight, although it was a fight with your hands tied behind your back. But over the past ten years, the cartels kept getting bigger and more powerful. They even have political clout now. The feds threw their hands up, gave a press conference, and called it an epidemic. Fighting an epidemic was a lot like eating an elephant. One bite at a time, brother. I'd start with Lee Chapman.

I imagined the guy got his jollies playing around with skulls and shaking tambourines, like some Palo Mayombe cheerleader, intimidating his victims and enemies. Probably picked up the tricks of the trade when he was at the Walls Unit in Huntsville. Chapman was a career criminal, who spent the majority of his life locked up. His rap sheet was like used toilet paper. Huntsville should have fried him.

It was bigger and better in the Lone Star State, including the execution chamber in Huntsville. That shake-and-bake was the most active in the country. And there was one simple reason that was so. You don't mess with Texas. Not our kids, women, or animals. Justice here was swift and deadly. My plan was to root Chapman out like the vermin he was and exterminate him. *Adios*, Lee Chapman.

My blood pressure was up this morning, thinking about my last phone call from Hannah and Nocona. They came within seconds of each other. They shared one name, Lee Chapman. The entire case changed at that moment. This wasn't an epidemic where I was going to hang my head low and whine like the feds. No, I was preparing for war. After all these years in law enforcement, I knew to trust my gut. Here was every atom in my body, millions of years old, telling me to hunt Chapman down till I dropped him.

I left the deputy behind with Dolores in the office because I didn't need any clowns tagging along to Hannah's place. Nocona was meeting me there. I wondered if he'd bring that border agent he was sleeping with. I could punch him for complicating this investigation by making her part of the team. The entire investigation was a cluster of federal agents, local law enforcement, and hocus-pocus. It was everything I tried to avoid from the get-go.

The unknowns and what-ifs had my gut on fire, so I chewed a few antacids and washed them down with a cold Styrofoam cup of coffee. I slowly inhaled and exhaled when I got to Hannah's gate. I didn't need to wind her up any further than she already was. She rambled on the phone about an old woman with cataracts walking the land. Hell, that was a twist in the weirdness, but I'd known Hannah most of my life. She wasn't a liar. You get to my age and work a job like this, you begin to realize perception is reality for most people. Hannah believed Jesus was in her heart and the devil was under her heel. My religion was simple—good and evil existed in all men and women. I didn't learn that from the Bible. I learned that from living.

I pulled up next to Nocona's truck parked in the drive. Bet he was already inside playing the respectful Marine, the mystical Comanche, rolling himself into a perfect border agent burrito. Wonder what he thought of that old woman on Hannah's property?

Hannah's two dogs greeted me. June was a friendly girl marking her time on the front porch. She didn't even bother to meet me at the truck. She lifted her head and wagged her tail. She knew who I was, but Jack ran toward me, barking as soon as I slammed the truck door. He smelled bad news all over me. That dog growled low and mean when I tried to pet him. Odd for a hundred-pound Lab who knew me. Then I remembered. Not only was Jack the lead dog out here, but he had also been out with Hannah when she saw that old woman.

Good dogs had a heightened sense when it came to protecting property and their people. I found a reliable animal was much better than people at picking up clues cast off by dangerous people and situations. Horses had it, same as dogs. Jack was spooked.

"It's a big mess we're in, Jack," I moved slowly to him,

crouching down to his level and extending my right hand slowly, opened palm, until I saw him relax. I gave him a good rub behind his ears and along his torso. I stood up and saw Hannah on the porch.

"Sheriff, please come in. I made biscuits this morning with a side of sausage. Hope you're hungry."

I walked past the living room, where a dark-headed girl was sitting on the couch. She was wrapped up tightly in a crocheted afghan blanket of orange, brown, and yellow. The scene was straight out of a seventies playbook. It was too hot outside for a girl to be indoors covered up like it was winter. She began rocking back and forth when she noticed me. It stopped me cold. Strange girl, I thought. My gut said she was on the run from Chapman. Hannah turned around and stood next to me.

"Nocona's in the kitchen. You'll meet Ava soon enough."

"I'll take a couple of biscuits with sausage, Hannah," I said, following her into the kitchen. "How you doing this morning, Agent Ketemoczy?"

He looked up at me with bloodshot eyes.

"Had a big time in Del Rio last night?"

"Sheriff, what I do on my own time is my business. Shut up with the sophomoric innuendos."

"Gentlemen, we're not going to have that kind of talk in this house on a Sunday morning," Hannah said, placing a plate of hot biscuits and sausage patties before me on the table. "We have plenty of work to do. Yesterday, I had quite a conversation with the young lady in the living room. We all know the man's name who hurt her."

"I apologize, ma'am," replied Nocona, looking directly at me.

I smiled at him to keep him on the defense. He quickly took the lead.

"I've been working with another agent in Del Rio on this case. She shared some intel about gang activity along the border. Tren de Aragua is a Venezuelan gang, been trafficking drugs in Texas for a few years. What makes them relevant to our case is that they dismember their enemies in the same manner we've found some of the victims. I don't think Tren de Aragua has a tie to Palo Mayombe, but I suspect Lee Chapman does as a means to intimidate victims," Nocona said.

"No shit, Sherlock," I said. Nocona shot me a side glance at that one.

"Ronnie, please," Hannah said, sitting down at the table next to Nocona. "Ava has a tattoo of a black cauldron with sticks. I looked up some things about Palo Mayombe on the internet. Ava's tattoo matches the ones I saw on several websites. When she told me about Lee Chapman earlier, she shook with fear. Whether the occult is real or not to us, Ava believes it. If you interview her today, I want to be sitting next to her."

"That's not a problem," I said, taking charge of this mess. "I've worked with you before, Hannah. I can trust you. Don't know if I can say the same for Nocona and his gal pal in Del Rio."

"She has a name, sheriff. Jo McKenney," Nocona replied, shooting me the stink eye. "I served with her in Afghanistan. I've trusted her more than once with my life. Good enough for you, sheriff?"

"All right now, Nocona. Settle down. I apologize for my smart remark."

"She's doing surveillance of a ranch located outside the city limits. She saw some human skulls and cauldrons with animal or human bones. There are also locked shipping containers out there. For now, she's working alone, without reporting back to the Highway 90 border patrol station. What do you think about that, sheriff?" said Nocona, hot under the collar and hung over. I was beginning to feel a little sorry for him.

"Looks like she's got some skin in the game. I appreciate that," I said, drinking the last of my coffee. "Look, the first step is following the money. There's always a trail. Who's writing the checks to Chapman? We need the jefe in this operation. You think Ava could help us with that, Hannah?"

"Yes, but before we talk to her, sheriff, there's something else I need to mention. I told you about the old woman walking around out here. She spoke to me, plain as day, so I know I'm not imagining her. I may be an old woman, but my mind is sharp. I can't help thinking this old woman is somehow involved. She didn't show up until I noticed that strange tattoo on Ava's arm."

A puff of air escaped from Nocona's lips. He was immediately embarrassed by it, hiding his recognition of the old woman behind his sudden interest in drinking cold coffee.

"I heard that, Nocona," I said. "What's up with this old woman? You know her?"

Hannah and I both stared at him, waiting for an answer. Nocona finally stood and walked over to the kitchen window. He spoke low and carefully.

"I met her a long time ago when I was a kid in Mexico. I don't know much else about her. She worked in the Sonora witches' market selling religious icons and telling fortunes. She always appears to me when something bad is about to happen."

"You're not making any sense," I said in disbelief. "What? She just appears, like a ghost, or is she some freak stalking you?"

"The witch of Sonora has been following me for years. If Hannah has seen her, then things are about to get a lot worse."

"Is she a threat?" I wouldn't let him off the hook. I could

tell by his folded arms across his chest he was trying to shut this conversation down. "Is she even real? Does she have a name? An address?"

"Don't talk to her, Hannah," Nocona said, once again ignoring me. "I'll take care of her."

"What?" I said, crossing my arms. "Are you going to arrest her? What for? Arrest an old woman for being creepy? Maybe for trespassing, but come on, Nocona. We need to stay focused on Chapman."

"I should have done it a long time ago," Nocona said to Hannah.

"What the hell does that even mean, you'll take care of her? Are you planning on killing that old woman?"

"I said I'd take care of it, sheriff."

"Please, lower your voices," Hannah said in a demanding voice that brought us to her attention. "Think of that poor girl in the other room." Hannah picked up the empty plate in front of me and walked it over to the kitchen sink. She returned and stood next to Nocona, who hadn't moved an inch from the window.

"Nocona, you must listen to me," Hannah said. "The witch is an unclean spirit. She follows you because she knows something deep within you. Something that makes you vulnerable to her. Maybe it's something you did or some sort of pain you carry, like a generational pain."

Nocona was speechless. He kept looking at Hannah and the doorway leading out. I don't know if he was looking for an escape route, but Hannah laid him wide open.

"Don't be afraid of her," Hannah continued. "She'll only feed on that, on your fear. Like Jesus in the synagogue, in Capernaum, casting out the evil spirits within a man. You must fight her. With all your spirit. But you won't be able to do that until you've looked deep within your own soul. Heal the pain you carry, Nocona. A pain that comes from your father, grandfather, and great-grandfather. All who suffered before you. The witch knows this, and she uses it against you. She will never stop feeding off your pain until you recognize what is causing that pain inside of you."

That was one hell of a sermon for a Sunday morning. Nocona was clearly shaken.

"Thank you, ma'am. Sheriff, I'll be in touch regarding the ranch in Del Rio."

He wasn't out of the kitchen for more than a second, when Hannah and I heard him say, "The girl's gone."

CHAPTER THIRTEEN

Lee Chapman
Ranch near Canyon Rim
Del Rio, Texas

I'm a Florida cracker, born and bred in Ocala, along the Mason-Dixon line between the panhandle and the peninsula. Four syllables in that word—peninsula. I'm not a moron, though plenty of people wrote me off as one. Never met my pa and had a crazy drunk for a ma. I spent my childhood with strangers in foster care.

I never did too good at school. Teachers and counselors said I was behavioral and learning disabled. Stamped it in red on every document I was ever mentioned in. I couldn't help but think having my head busted open at the bottom of an empty swimming pool didn't help much. I was just a little fella when I took a stroll out the open door of our ground-floor apartment and straight to the pool. At the time, Ma was sleeping one off. From the swimming-pool accident, I went lickety-split into foster care. For my future aspects, I realized right off the bat, there'd be no passing go and collecting two hundred bucks just 'cause I was a foster kid. That money was for the foster ma and pa.

Institutional livin' and bad headaches were what I got from my day at the pool. When my head started throbbing like it was clamped shut in a vise, I had to release it, or it would've exploded. I worked those headaches just like a pressure valve, slowly easing my pain away then handing it off to somebody else. When I was done, my head clicked shut, and I didn't feel a damn thing. That was why I had to hurt people.

The look of shock in a woman's eyes when I cut her made that deep throbbing inside my head stop. When she cried and begged me to leave her alone or to let her die, well, it was better than a bottle of Tylenol or Bayer.

It shouldn't be that simple for me, but it was. My pain stopped when theirs began. My heaven became their hell. Share and share alike, brothers and sisters!

I never could stand the way people fumbled blindly through their lives without any pain, living in a big-ass house with a mom and dad, vacations with Mickey in Orlando. They never deserved any of it. The fools thought that was what they deserved. People like me weren't on their radar screen. I wasn't worth a dime in their world. But I was gonna even the score. Their god never offered to do it. Uncle Sam sure wasn't up to it, but I knew I could even the score. I was a winner, baby!

I was fifteen years old when I robbed the 7-Eleven three blocks from my foster family's house. When I was all alone one sunny morning, I borrowed the SIG hidden underneath the towels in the bathroom. It felt good having that gun in my pocket, like I was in control of my life for the very first time. I kept patting it like a lucky rabbit's foot.

Once I got to the 7-Eleven, I stood outside and waited for the last customer to walk out. I peeked through the glass door, and there was one woman standing behind the counter. I strolled in like I owned the place, went behind the counter, and hit her on the side of the head with the gun. Her mouth was wide open with an expression of shock that I had actually done what I just did. I called her a stupid cow and gave her another whack until she dropped cold to the floor. Blood spurted from her head in two places. It was weird looking.

I had enough time to clean out the register and make myself a Slurpee. I strolled out of the 7-Eleven, drinking my Slurpee with a wad of cash in one pocket and the gun in the other. Easy day.

The next thing I knew, I hitched a ride with a fat trucker headed to San Diego. With thirty-six hours of drive time, I convinced him I was an abused teen, running from a bad home. Jimbo had that same sad story, though he never served time in foster care. The worst he got as a kid was being whipped on a regular schedule with a razor strap by his step-daddy. I would have choked that SOB with that strap and stuffed it down his throat until he choked. I told Jimbo so. I think he appreciated that.

I never felt like hurting Jimbo; my head didn't hurt when we were sitting high in that big truck looking down on people below. I felt free in the cab, saying goodbye to school and fake-as-shit foster mamas and daddies who couldn't wait to get their monthly check.

I liked to listen when Jimbo talked to other truckers all over the country. They were like family. He let me talk to them too. His friends never treated me like I was a dumbass.

Jimbo was good to me, and I felt like I had a real friend for the first time in my life. He fed me and broke up the ride with a stay at a La Quinta Inn. I've never stayed in a motel, so it was pure luxury to me: two king-sized beds, big-screen TV, and pancakes for breakfast. My only complaint for the time I spent with him was that he reeked of BO. That, and he talked too damn much. He made my ears tired, listening to the same stories over and over again.

When he dropped me off near Interstate 8 in San Diego, he handed me three Franklins and the jacket he was wearing. Within two days I had a job trafficking heroin and cocaine from Tijuana to San Diego, working for a small cartel in Baja.

The boss man liked my method with a hammer in discouraging cheaters and deceivers. The first blow went to the elbow, which sent the idjit straight to his knees. The second blow was to the back of the head. End of story. Another happy ending for me and the boss man. He used to tell me I was a boy after his own heart.

Eventually, I got busted in LA County for running a special package to a big shot who lived on the west side, up in the hills. It was a big house with one of those infinity pools perched high above the little people below. It reminded me a lot of being in that eighteen-wheeler with Jimbo. I thought I recognized a few faces from TV when I met my man, but I was in and out of there quick, just like my arrest a mile from the place, quick. Then lickety-split, I was off to jail.

Maybe I was set up by low men on the totem pole in the organization. I was a skinny white kid who was running circles around them, plus the boss man loved me. Any-who, I was charged with transporting cocaine across two county lines with an intent to sell. I swear to this day, the big shot who lived in the house with the fancy-ass pool never served time for dealing drugs. Those dudes never do.

I ended up serving three years in some crappy juvey detention center. I could have gotten out earlier because I was a juvey with no police record and a homeless boy. But the headaches returned. Being locked in a cage most of the day didn't help my disposition. I punched a guard, broke a counselor's nose, and dislocated a teacher's shoulder when the vise got too tight around my head.

When I got out, thanks to a hookup from a fellow inmate, I moved to Galveston. That's where I began working for the Jalisco New Generation Cartel, distributing cocaine, fentanyl, heroin, meth, you name it, throughout Galveston and Houston. That's also where I got a new hammer, a bigger one this time. One that wouldn't break.

I worked that job for four years until cops busted us up in 2020. Like cockroaches, we scrambled to get out of the area. But those Houston cops, man, they knew the streets better than the rats in the sewers. Once the feds started the indictments, I got charged with trafficking four hundred grams of meth, a first-degree felony with five years—hello, Huntsville!

It was there at the Walls I learned about Palo Mayombe, mumbo jumbo, hocus-pocus. My cellie thought his religion gave him protection and special powers like some sort of magician or witch doctor. Marco said he picked it up in Miami, when he was smuggling Cubans from the Puerto de Mariel into Dade County. He swore to me he never had an ounce of trouble at the Walls, especially from the Aryan Brotherhood of Texas. The Brothers were always on the lookout for new peckerwoods to do their dirty work.

Marco sported a huge tat on his throat of a cauldron, skull, and bird talons. People left him the hell alone. You had to be some kind of badass to walk around a prison like a free bird. You either had to join a gang or became so evil no one wanted you around. So, I signed up with my Palo Mayombe brethren and got a tat like my cellie. Unlike Marco, though, I served all my time.

Being locked up like a mangy dog brought those headaches back. The bigger the headaches got, the more I wanted a release, one that was hot and mean. I wanted to crush the life out of someone, hurt 'em with the same kind of pain I felt. I was entitled, just like everybody else, to pain-free living.

I spent most of my time perfecting my Spanish with tapes and headphones in the prison library and learned everything I could about Palo Mayombe. It was nothing more than a card trick for me with a ceremony and music—all the trappings any religion had. I used it to my advantage, just like any preacher of the Word. I intimidated people, and they left me the hell alone in the Walls. Every day I honed my magic. Every day I thought about returning to the Jalisco New Generation Cartel. Every day I made and sorted my plans.

That day finally came. I worked the border, trafficking girls and drugs until El Jefe asked me to set up shop in Del Rio. It was a bonus, considering I was one of five white guys in the entire operation. I paid cash for a brand-new satellite phone and a big Texas man ranch near Seminole Canyon State Park. I got busy moving the shipping containers, drug mules, and cauldrons there. I was assembling the circus with the help of a few chickadees, but they tried to fly away. I found two and spanked them hard. Little Ava was still out there. I'd find her. She deserved a spanking too.

I've always liked the desert. Hot and unforgiving. You couldn't be an idjit out here. You'd fry. The mornings were the best, though. Early morning, right before the sun came up, the coyotes yelped from the canyons. They were hungry, just like everyone on this planet. Some expected eggs and bacon, whether they deserved it or not. Some got a crumb from The Man, because they were cowards. Not me. I made my way, taking what I wanted. I was a winner, baby!

CHAPTER FOURTEEN

Nocona Ketemoczy
Rocksprings, Texas

When I walked out of Hannah's kitchen and saw Ava was gone, I began tracking her shoe prints from the front door to the entrance gate of the ranch. It was easy enough following the flip-flops she wore, with their faint prints on the dry caliche dirt. But once she stepped over the cattle guard, there was nothing to track. No imprints, no brush pushed aside near a fence post she might have tried to cross. Nothing. It was as if she had vanished into thin air. I wondered if she went back to Chapman. It wasn't the first time I'd been reminded that the devil you know is better than the one you don't know.

She might have hidden a cell phone at the shelter, so communication with the people she ran with was possible. Two facts stood out: The sight of the sheriff in uniform and our arguing in the kitchen made her run.

Being deported or incarcerated as a drug trafficker was far

worse in Ava's mind than being with Lee Chapman. She was running for her life with nowhere to go except where she started.

I'm sure Ava heard the heated discussion about the witch and her own ties to Palo Mayombe. The sheriff had his assumptions about the witch, but Hannah knew exactly what was up. The witch of Sonora was feeding on my pain. Pain coded into my DNA and my time as a Marine.

Hannah said my pain was generational. You think? I played the game of things not being fair since I realized I had a huge deficit—Mexican and Comanche mixed breed born and bred in Texas. Drank like a crazy man and wrecked a lot of cars after learning about all the federally mandated acts of the nineteenth and twentieth centuries that created genocide against the American Indian. I was never forgiving or forgetting the institutionalization of Indian children at the schools run by Christians and the government. It had been a slow burn for me since I was a teenager.

Of course, there was a final gut punch in all this madness. It took over a hundred years for this country, some churches, even Canada to apologize for the marked and unmarked burial sites of children found behind those schools.

So, I pushed that generational pain as far back as I could, knowing it would only raise its ugly head again. I eventually quit drinking and wrecking cars as a means of fighting the pain. Realizing I needed self-discipline before I killed myself or someone else on the road or in a bar, I joined the Marines and channeled all that pain into rage against the enemy. I was a damn good Marine.

For the tribesmen who couldn't run from their pain, they marked their days on the res with alcohol, violence, and drugs. Smelling blood, the cartels moved in quickly with meth and fentanyl. A few years ago, Indian Tribal Police and leaders met with the Interior Department to combat the onslaught. Later, the Oglala Sioux at Pine Ridge Res declared a state of emergency. Yeah, The Man was still trying to kill us.

These thoughts played in my head while I continued searching the ranch and surrounding area until two that morning. I was spent, physically and mentally, so I headed back to town. I slept, despite my dreams, until five.

Halloween morning dawned outside my bedroom window with a view of the witch. She was leaning against my truck in the parking lot, pointing her finger in the direction of the sky above her. I looked above me and saw the sun struggling to push its rays through a ragged band of cumulus clouds. Then the witch turned her milky eyes toward me and laughed.

The remnants of a Cat 3 hurricane that hit north of Corpus Christi was making its way through San Antonio into the Hill Country. A cluster was forming with a blue norther blowing in from the northwest with strong winds and black skies. I've known those fast-moving cold fronts to drop the temperature by thirty degrees in minutes.

This area always needed rain, but it couldn't handle flash flooding with dry terrain of thin topsoil and exposed rocks and boulders. Couple that with all of the river crossings being very low. Flash flooding was deadly here. I was home in Bandera in July 1987 when ten children from a nearby summer camp drowned trying to escape the floodwaters. Their camp bus was washed away in the raging Guadalupe River. When the water came off the surrounding hills, it was always fast and lethal.

I was driving to the field office when the clouds burst open, sending pounding rain across the windshield. Watching the wiper blades' motion, my mind drifted to Jo. I hadn't texted or called her since we'd been together. I felt bad about that, reassuring myself I'd do it once I was in the office, but the road to hell is paved with good intensions. I hoped I hadn't hurt her with my silence.

Before the storm increased, I drove out to the crossroads, one only the devil could inspire, and placed a few remotely monitored seismic sensors while looking for migrants. People had been there, leaving empty water bottles behind them and plastic grocery bags blowing in the dust. Then I headed to Highway 377, following the West Llano River into Junction. My gut told me Ava had followed the river as a means of staying out of sight and connecting to Interstate 10 outside of Junction.

The rain intensified, making it difficult for the wiper blades to keep up. Several times the truck skidded along the snaky route with its hairpin curves. I slowed it down to a cautious thirty-five, allowing myself to think of happier times I'd spent on this same road with my dad. The family would have a picnic at the nearby state park while Dad and I slipped off to do some fly-fishing.

The Llano River was a tributary of the Colorado River, where parts of the Edwards Plateau drained into the rolling limestone terrain. Spring fed, the North and South Llano eventually joined in Junction before heading north of Enchanted Rock, a sacred place of the Comanche. To fish on that river with my dad meant a lot. We caught bluegills there on a rare, carefree day we spent together. Otherwise, he was working.

The truck windows started to fog up. The front hit strong. I pulled off at one of the kayak-launching sites along the river to take a look around. Once out of the truck, I realized the temp must have dropped twenty degrees, with a hard wind pushing the rain in all directions. Its pellets stung my face and hands.

I would have liked to walk around and spy a few Rio Grande turkeys roosting near the river, but not a chance in this weather. I had to shake my nostalgia and stop thinking of Dad. The possibility of a life with Jo was distracting me as well. In this job and my job as a Marine, tenderness got you killed. My dad was gone, and Jo was a luxury I wouldn't allow myself. I had to find Ava before Chapman did.

CHAPTER FIFTEEN

Jo McKenney
Del Rio, Texas

Chalk it up to I should have known better. I wasn't twenty anymore, sitting by the phone, willing it to ring. I couldn't really say I was a seasoned player. I still believed, which is what made me hurt so damn bad. The first day I knew he'd call me after work and say he couldn't wait to see me again. But that wasn't happening. The more time passed, the more it sank in deeper—I was an idiot to make a friend a lover. It was a cold hard fact that should be tattooed on my heart.

And I did the same old thing I've always done when my heart was broken. I listened to Kelly Willis, drank too much wine, and cried myself to sleep. The next morning, I got into my Teflon-coated agent uniform and wrote Nocona off. He wasn't getting any more kisses, tears, or time from me.

By ten the next morning, I replayed every movement we made and every word we spoke at the restaurant and at the house. All his charms were laid out before me at the restaurant

—the quiet man with dark eyes and straight black hair staring at my earrings and dress. He was eager to please, wearing his new shirt and smiling at me from across the table, because he was hoping I liked what I saw. I had always loved what I saw in him, from the intelligent professional who cared about his job and respected my opinion to the handsome man who was often shy and withdrawn.

But the greatest charm this man had for this woman was the way he kissed me goodbye after we woke up the next morning, shy and a bit scared, wondering what we had gotten ourselves into. He reassured me our time together was something solid when he pulled back my hair in one hand and put the other hand on the side of my face and kissed me. He held me like I was the most precious, fragile thing in the world to him. No man ever kissed me like that. I had it bad, and I just couldn't tell my heart to stop thinking of him.

I went back to making up excuses for him because I wanted to believe there was an excuse. I knew extreme weather was moving into the area. It didn't take much for the Hill Country to flood, making roads and bridges a washout. But those cell towers were still standing, and the Rocksprings agent office was still operating. That office didn't have half the responsibilities the Del Rio agency had. Working too much was a poor excuse for him because his job was nothing compared to where I worked and what was expected of us as border agents.

The Del Rio Sector covered 245 miles along the Rio Grande River and Lake Amistad. We were responsible for 55,000-plus miles of Texas in forty-seven counties. Although it was mostly farms and ranches, the job was overwhelming. We were a Band-Aid on trafficking and a revolving door on immigration.

People hated us for being border agents. We hated ourselves for a job that rarely made a difference. Oh, I had my glory days uniting children with their families. It gave me a thrill to hold a trafficker at gunpoint. But every day I began this job with a vision of Sisyphus pushing a boulder up a hill, only to have it roll back down again. That was the itinerary, and it never, ever changed. It was a lot like being a soldier in Afghanistan. You wanted to believe you were helping the children and women there. They could go to school and learn once you cleared out the bad guys. But the next day the Taliban moved in, burned down the school, and killed the kids. I'm a former ranger. A snake eater. But day after day of a failed mission eats your soul.

Noco had his own head games with Afghanistan. He was perpetually stuck in moral injury although he'd never talk about it. And I was too afraid of asking him. What little time we had spent together the past few years was mostly about agent work and a little about enjoying each other as a man and woman, not as agents, not as soldiers. Those hours were too few.

Soldiers learned to limp along for years with mental wounds. A lot of them buried the pain with self-medication. That medicine was found in booze, sex, exercise, whatever it took to numb the pain. If you couldn't get away from the pain, you'd blow your brains out. I never knew how close Noco was to the last solution. I just couldn't break down that wall he'd built years ago. God, I wanted to, I wanted to love that man, but he refused to let me.

Our mission in Afghanistan began with work in the mountains. The terrain was tough, but the weather was worse. In one day, you could walk in a temp range from forty degrees to ninety. The higher we climbed, the more we realized the enemy was looking at us from above. Our come-to-Jesus moment had arrived.

We had received intel of a mujahideen warlord's home in that location. He was operating much like the cartel bosses do today. Actually, it was the exact MO as the cartels with forced recruitment of men and boys, the murder of locals as an example of their power and taking villagers' money at gunpoint. Our mission was to neutralize the warlord at the top of the hill.

Once we were in position, Noco tossed several M67s into the compound. When the smoke from the grenades cleared, the thug and his family were killed, eleven children in total. We could have ripped our hearts out and buried them with the children, but Noco—oh, God, I'll never forget his face. He was in shock, waving his hands in the air, screaming "No!" over and over again. He refused to let anyone touch the bodies in preparation for burial; at times he threatened to shoot us if we got involved. He buried all eleven children, and we watched him in our trained silence as soldiers, grieving for the loss of innocent lives and the agony of our brother, Noco. He still carried it, the guilt, it was all there in his eyes. I doubted he ever slept a full night. I'm sure mornings rarely offered a reason to get up.

The surveillance work I did at Canyon Rim was the reason I got up this morning. I decided to take the Jeep, instead of the issued agent truck. It was easier to hide what I was doing from the boss and Chapman. The minute the cartel-paid locals saw a border agent truck making its rounds, they'd let their man know. The criminal network had many tentacles out here. Once the news was out, you were a direct target.

Spooky to think, I was headed out there on Halloween with the torture-chamber shipping containers and shelves full of skulls. But I was hanging fire on this mission. I had to get out of my funk by relying on myself. I wasn't sitting around waiting for marching orders from no man.

My AOR was the weirdo's ranch. I'd been watching him for days, walking around, talking to himself. I'd shut down that airstrip of his, along with the shipments of fentanyl. I was talking tough, but my mind kept returning to Noco. I wished I could say he was the reason I started this day.

Sunny Shelly, my mom, was in my head telling me not to give up. "Cook him a nice meal, Josie. Wear something pretty." Mama still believed the dating rules of the twentieth century worked in this century. I know it hurt her asking because God, how I hated hearing her say, "Honey, you need to think about getting married and starting a family. It's time to get out of the military and start a life for yourself." The questions became more urgent once I hit thirty. *Mama, I just can't find the right man. Maybe I'm not the right woman.* For a long time, I stopped caring. I just worked to eat up the days and nights, but seeing Noco, touching him—he made me believe. That hope thing was a killer. Every damn time.

Riding along the river, I thought of the hiking trips I took near Seminole Canyon State Park when I first moved here. I loved the colors in the fall. The green of the river. The rust and orange of the Presa and upper canyons. Noco would have loved this place. I sipped the pumpkin-spiced coffee I paid too much for and made myself sad thinking about the what-ifs.

I finished my coffee right before turning off onto a dirt road. I parked the Jeep out of view, then walked the rest of the way to a group of boulders to do surveillance of the ranch. I had to focus. The job was too dangerous not to. *No more man in my head*, I told myself when I adjusted the .40-caliber pistol on my hip. I carried an M4 rifle with a silencer across my person. The last thing I remembered before blacking out was silencing my cell phone and shoving it between two rocks.

When I came to, I had a huge headache. I touched the back of my head and felt blood and clumps of hair on my shoulder and neck. Once my eyes focused in the dim light coming from cracks in the wooden shed and holes in the tin roof, I saw my feet trapped in wooden stocks. A heavy metal chain was wrapped around my neck, and my mouth was bound in duct tape. *Damn it, man.* It was my own fault for creating this situation. I told myself not to panic and began zeroing in on getting the hell out of here. The chain around my neck made it difficult for me to look for an exit. To conserve my energy, I became very still. Outside I could hear two women laughing.

As if on cue, the devil himself opened the door.

"Good morning. Hope you find your accommodations comfortable. Oh, that's right. You can't talk or move much," Chapman laughed. "Don't know if you're a classic movie buff. But this place is modeled after the sweatbox in *Cool Hand Luke* with Paul Newman. Probably made before you was born. It's a prison drama set in the Deep South. But down in Duval County, Florida, the sweatbox was the real deal for a lot of prisoners at the Sunbeam Prison Camp. Hell of a name for a prison, don't you think?"

He stood in front of me and kicked me repeatedly in the stomach.

"I know what prison life is like. I thought you might like a taste," he said before walking through the small door into the blinding heat of the day.

Focus. Focus, I told myself over and over again as I stared at that door in front of me, waiting for him to walk through it again.

CHAPTER SIXTEEN

Hannah Durand
Casa de Katia
Rocksprings, Texas

With the rain and wind getting worse by the hour, I told Elizabeth we'd celebrate Halloween early with the girls. I hated to complain about the rain since we'd been in a drought for several years, but when it flooded here, the creeks and rivers quickly rose, making the river crossings dangerous. We had plenty of groceries to last us for several days. There'd be no reason to leave the ranch.

There were a few decorations in the kitchen the girls hung up earlier. Accordion-bodied skeletons danced from a string. Plastic bats flew from the ceiling fan blades, and black spiders climbed their white webs around the window frames. I moved the girls' jack-o'-lanterns from the front porch to the kitchen table once the rain set in. All of it created a festive mood, keeping our minds off of Ava if only for an hour or two. I was worried sick, constantly checking my phone to see if Nocona or the sheriff had texted me.

I only had five girls to feed now that Ava was gone. I put on a pot of chili midmorning for our hot dogs. Elizabeth had diced the onions for me earlier. I would have never put out a jar of store-bought pickle relish when I was younger, but there it was on the counter by the hot dog buns. August had always loved homemade chow-chow relish. The more peppers in the relish, the better he liked it.

Elizabeth went home a little after ten this morning, before the water rose. She had to drive into town and cross a few creeks before getting there. She'd wanted to see her grandchildren in their costumes even though there wouldn't be much trick-or-treating for the children in this weather. Most families just did a little party at home these days. It became too dangerous even in a little town to go door to door trick-or-treating. People didn't want to know who lived next door, much less have their children knock on the door. It was just another sign of the times.

I had plenty of help from Megan, so Elizabeth could enjoy her grands. Megan came to us about two years ago. She had been sex trafficked to work casinos in Mississippi and private parties when she was seventeen, right out of high school. She found out about Casa de Katia from stickers we had placed in motel rooms on the bathroom mirrors. Our website and phone number were listed on the stickers. We had an army of volunteers who made sure those stickers were in every motel along the I-10 corridor from San Antonio to Jacksonville, Florida.

Megan rode a bus to Rocksprings from Biloxi, Mississippi, after finding out about us. I picked her up in front of the Lowe's Grocery Store on a cold February morning. I'll never forget that day. She was a pretty girl with long blond hair and sad eyes in a cheap parka with a broken zipper. Everything she owned was in a small purple suitcase and a bulging Walmart plastic bag.

She was leaning against a cart outside the grocery store, smoking a cigarette. I got out of the truck and walked straight to her. I asked if she was Megan Ladner, and she nodded.

"Ms. Hannah, thank you for coming to get me. I had to get out of Biloxi. Start living right," she said, dropping the cigarette to the ground and grinding it out with the tip of her shoe.

I immediately fell in love with her Southern drawl and manners. When I tried to carry her suitcase, she wouldn't let me.

"No, ma'am. I'm no lazy girl."

She put her suitcase in the back of the truck and closed the door. I offered her a cup of coffee from the thermos I brought with me. Next to the thermos was a paper bag with the egg and bacon sandwich I made when I got up this morning. I never knew what kind of shape these girls would be in when I picked them up. I just couldn't stand the thought of someone hungry in a land of plenty. Never could.

In between bites of the sandwich and sips of coffee, Megan told me her story. She didn't cry. I think she might have told it to a lot of people. I'm sure many used her story against her as a way to shame and control her. Maybe I was the first one to listen without an ulterior motive.

"I'm an Air Force brat, Ms. Hannah. My daddy was an enlisted man at Keesler. I'm from a big family with a daddy who stayed away as much as he could and a mama who had a lot on her plate. They fought like dogs, so the sooner I could get out of that house, the better."

She stopped talking long enough to eat her sandwich, then she thanked me for it.

"My daddy was getting relocated to Lackland in San

Antonio the month after I graduated from high school. I loved the beaches in Biloxi. I had good friends. So, I stayed behind working at Woody's Roadside as a waitress. My parents didn't care. I was one less kid to worry about."

I stared at the road in front of me, waiting for the very sad punchline I had heard many times of a vulnerable girl, a child really, left behind to make her own way.

"An old man, you'd never think he was bad, he looked just like Santa Claus. He came in the restaurant every day, always asking how I was doing and leaving a big tip. It was a month from high school graduation, so I was desperate for money. My best friend was bailing out on me to move in with her boyfriend, and I was nervous about the rent money. The old man, he told me to call him Jim, ended up being my best friend. He kept reassuring me everything was gonna be okay, even though I was broke. He at least listened and cared about my situation. I was very lonely then."

I turned toward her and nodded, encouraging her to continue.

"The restaurant visits from Jim lasted a couple of months until the day he asked me if I'd like to make some good money. He told me about some important people on the coast having a big party. All I had to do was serve food and drinks. He pulled out three one-hundred-dollar bills and set them on the table underneath the check for his meal. He then told me the address of the party and to wear a white blouse with black pants."

She paused and drank all of her coffee, staring out at the road in front of her.

"You're a Christian lady, Ms. Hannah. I don't want to offend you, so I'll just make this part quick. I went to that party, and I got drunk. I'm sure my drinks were spiked with Ambien. I had sex with a lot of men that night. I was so ashamed the next morning I wanted to die, but I didn't. So, I just took drugs and drank more alcohol and had sex with more men. For a couple of years, I moved around with Jim to New Orleans, Biloxi, and Jacksonville. Always the same. Always big parties with men. Always hating myself. When I saw Casa de Katia's phone number on a sticker in a motel room, I called when Jim was out getting us something to eat. I ran. I ran until I got here."

I pulled the truck off on the side of the road and walked around to her side of the truck. When I put my arms around her, she began to cry. I let her cry it out, standing outside the truck, listening to the mockingbirds call to each other from the pasture across the barbed-wire fence. When she stopped crying, I offered her another cup of coffee from the thermos. There was no need for more talking. I drove Megan home.

I loved her like a daughter. She was a blessing to me and Elizabeth with her hardworking, quiet ways. She's been on the payroll for about a year now. She'd be helping me today with the girls and making sure everyone was safe and sound in the bunkhouse later tonight.

I was expecting her any minute now when I heard her knock at the front door.

"Come on in, Megan."

She entered the kitchen with a smile on her face.

"You know you don't have to knock, sweetie. No need to be so formal."

"I know, Ms. Hannah. I'm just being polite."

She walked into the kitchen and pulled the flour, sugar, salt, and baking powder from the cupboard.

"Let me get the milk and eggs for you, Megan."

"I thought I'd use some orange food coloring for the cupcakes, Ms. Hannah. Make them look like little pumpkins. I can use candy corn for their eyes and mouth."

"The girls will love it."

She pulled out a large mixing bowl from the cabinet and started sifting the flour.

"Making two dozen, just because everyone here has a sweet tooth," she laughed.

We worked together in the kitchen for a few hours, then she walked over to the bunkhouse to get the girls for lunch. They arrived with hoodies and light jackets on to ward off the rain and chill. With the hot dogs, chili, and sides, it wasn't long until all the girls were laughing and eating. It was always a joy to have people in my kitchen, breaking bread together.

There were a few large cracks of lightning as we ate. The girls would jump up from the table to look out the kitchen window. The wind was blowing hard now. A few times the kitchen lights blinked.

"Ladies, we may be dining by candlelight soon," I said.

Megan and I got out all the candles and the hurricanes lamps from the cupboard while the girls finished their plates. Megan cleared the table for me.

"I'm going to show you all how to light the hurricane lamps. You need to be careful and not drop it. Not only would the glass shatter, but you could spill kerosene. It's very flammable."

I demonstrated how to use the lamps. Then I had Megan box up all the cupcakes, candles, and hurricanes lamps to take to the bunkhouse.

"Girls, now don't be afraid. Megan has been with us a while and knows just what to do in case we lose power. If we do, it doesn't take long for Pedernales Co-op to get things on again. Y'all can take your jack-o'-lanterns with you. Just be careful with open flames when lighting the candles inside."

It was a short party, but I got a good hug from all of the girls before they left. I needed to get a walk in with Jack before it got any worse out there. June refused to go out when it was raining, but Jack loved his walks in all kinds of weather, especially when it rained. A true Labrador, Jack loved water. There was no mud puddle left alone when he was out walking. I put on a raincoat and my boots and headed out the door once I saw all the girls had made it to the bunkhouse.

Jack led me past the windmill with its blades spinning wildly. It scared me to think one could break and fly off, hitting an animal or the nearby barn. Jack increased the pace, and I was eager to get our walk over and done. We walked about another yard or two, when the driving rain pelted my face, smarting my skin. I pulled the hood of the raincoat tighter against me and tucked my chin as close as I could underneath it to protect my skin.

"Do your business, Jack, and let's go home."

He veered to the left of me into some high bluegrass plumes, bending back and forth in the wild wind. His usual habit was to go off in tall grass to poop. *It won't be long now*, I thought to myself. I longed for a hot cup of tea in my warm kitchen.

When Jack hadn't returned, I thought he might have caught sight of a squirrel or jackrabbit and decided to give the poor animal a good chase. I stood beneath the shelter of an old oak tree, waiting for him. I could see by its stripped branches that the bucks were in velvet. The hairy growth on their antlers was itchy, so they rubbed them against tree bark or branches until they were stripped bare. The males of the species were not shy about making their presence known. After they rubbed their antlers, they'd paw the ground with their hooves and pee to mark their spot.

I whistled for Jack. It was time to go. My body was shaking from the sudden temperature drop from the norther.

"Jack. Come on, boy, let's go."

"Hannah."

I recognized her voice and turned around to face the evil calling my name. The wind and rain were driving so hard I could barely see in front of me.

"Hannah."

I walked toward her. I would not show her I was afraid.

"Get out of here," I screamed in the wind. "Leave this land and these girls alone. Nocona realizes now you're nothing more than a powerless spirit, feeding off of him. No one is afraid of you."

I still couldn't see her, but I could hear her wild laughter. I walked quickly in that direction, hunched from the rain and cold.

"Come closer, Hannah. We need to talk."

I followed the voice, walking more quickly, still not seeing her, blinded by the rain.

"Jack. Get over here, Jack."

I couldn't even see my hands in front of me, let alone my dog, but it didn't stop me from walking toward the witch's voice. Like the foolish old woman I was, I tripped over a large piece of limestone, hitting my head on it before falling down. I touched the back of my head and felt the blood.

"Stupid old fool," laughed the witch.

"Jack." I continued calling my dog. I was afraid he couldn't see me here on the ground. I tried to pick myself up. My body just wasn't working. Between the weather and arthritis, I was in a bad way. I got on my knees and crawled a few feet, thinking I could right myself if I could grab hold of a bush or a low-lying branch.

I felt dizzy, so I stopped struggling to crawl. I needed to save what little energy I had so I could eventually muster the strength to stand up. The rain pelted my body, so I curled up on one side with my arms and legs drawn into my chest. I could maintain my body heat if I stayed that way.

To my enemy, I am sure I looked like a wounded animal on the ground. Vulnerable and defenseless. It probably made the witch feel more powerful. But this was temporary, I told myself again and again, repeating the same phrases like a prayer. *Don't give into the pain, Hannah. Meet this evil spirit head on. You are stronger.*

I forced myself to open my eyes in the blinding rain. I saw her shoes, black pointed boots, close to my face. I could almost touch the hem of her dress, ripped and covered in mud from where she dragged it across the land.

I closed my eyes and began praying for the strength to get up and meet her head on. I wasn't going to die this way, at her feet. But the more I struggled to sit up, the weaker I felt.

"Where's your Jesus, Hannah?" The witch laughed.

With everything in me, I pulled myself up, grabbing on to the filthy dress she wore. The fabric began to give, but not before I was able to stand.

"In the name of Jesus, I rebuke you."

The witch raised her fist against me, knocking me back down.

"'For we wrestle not against flesh and blood, but against principalities, against powers, against the rulers of the darkness of this world, against spiritual wickedness in high places,'" I shouted from *Ephesians* into the wind. "I am not afraid of you, witch."

She knelt down close to my face and blew a noxious fume over me, then she was gone. The blood from my head was now covering my neck and back. I knew I was dying. I felt my spirit slipping away with each breath I took. Then I heard a voice.

"Hannah, we've come to take you home."

I saw August, my sweet husband, standing by the big oak

tree where I waited for Jack just moments ago. Abby, our beautiful border collie, was with him.

"Take my hand, sweetheart," he said, walking toward me.

I raised my arm then I closed my eyes, feeling like I could finally rest, knowing August was here. Soon, I'd be in his arms again. I was leaving this world of pain and disappointment forever. I was going home.

CHAPTER SEVENTEEN

Sheriff Ronnie Hoffman
Edwards County, Texas

Hollywood couldn't have made a better horror movie than the nightmare we lived through on Halloween night. We worked all night, fielding calls of stuck motorists in rising creeks, cattle drowning in swollen ditches, and the washing-away of an entire RV park. A flash flood ripped vehicles and people from their camping sites, sweeping them away in the Llano, until a rock or tree stopped them. One man had climbed a nearby cypress tree, hoping to escape the floodwaters. His clothing and skin were ripped from his body by the tree bark.

There was no way for us to get out and help people until the storm had passed or we'd drown like the rest of 'em. Those were hard calls to make. The Rocksprings Volunteer Fire Department was able to help some folks who were stranded thanks to the ladder truck they bought last year. In small towns, people either had to rely on themselves or a neighbor.

These days, most people didn't know the name of the person living a few feet from their front door.

The first call I had to return this morning was to Sheriff Tegler. Lack of sleep and anxiety over Ava's whereabouts had my mind stirred up, so I listened to the sheriff's phone message twice.

"I think we got your girl, Ronnie. Fits the image and description you sent. She was found near the river at Schreiner Park, right outside of Junction. She got caught on the rocks near the dam."

Ava. She must have followed the river road out of Rock-springs when she left Hannah's place. Poor girl thought she could walk all the way to Junction. She almost made it to the I-10 connection, where she would have been out of here forever. I sure didn't want to make that call to Hannah, but I was the only man standing. I'd drive in to Junction and confirm it was Ava, then touch base with Nocona. He could meet me out at Hannah's to deliver the news.

"Dolores, are we out of cheeseballs? Damn it to hell."

I hollered over to my administrative assistant, noticing two empty plastic containers on my desk.

"We've been out for a while, Ronnie. You never told me to get more."

"Dolores, if you see an empty container of cheeseballs, that means you should buy more."

I've always been a stress eater. Before that I was a smoker. My wife made me give up smoking. We were going to take a cruise on all the money we had saved from not buying cigarettes. No chance. Other bills came along and wiped out that little nest egg. But once I'm retired, we're going to take a cruise to the Caribbean. We'll get rum drinks with umbrellas. My life will no longer be eaten up by criminals and fools.

I was about to call Nocona when Elizabeth Gonzales

walked through my door. She looked bad. Now, I had had words with this woman before. She was no pushover. But one look at her, and I knew she'd been crying for hours.

"Liz, come on in. Sit down."

I pulled a chair out for her, and she collapsed into it.

"Ronnie, I found her this morning after the storm had passed. Megan called me earlier. No one could find her. They just didn't see her and Jack leave the ranch house for a walk. Maybe Hannah felt the need to get Jack out before the storm got worse," Liz said, clinging to a wet paper towel in her hand. "She must have fallen, Ronnie. She had a bad cut on the back of her head. Lots of blood. Oh, God, she wasn't that far from the house. Why didn't anyone hear her? I hate to think how long she lay in her own blood, calling out for help. Joseph is at the ranch now. We called for an ambulance. Ronnie, our beautiful Hannah is gone."

I stood up quickly. I felt like running through the door. Running out of this office, running somewhere that none of this was true. I walked over to Liz and wrapped my arms around her.

"Want me to drive you home, Liz?"

"No. I'll be all right, but somebody is going to have to call her son. That's why I'm here, 'cause it sure would have been easier to deliver this sad news over the phone. You know Joseph and me had a tough time with Sam and that snotty wife of his. It's obvious his wife hates Mexicans. They're probably going to think someone out here hurt her," she said, taking a breath, then wiping her eyes with the wadded paper towel. "You're the best one for the job, Ronnie. You've known her son since the day he was born. He at least will listen to you."

"I'll call Sam," I said, hoping to reassure her.

I walked her out of the office and stopped at Dolores's desk.

"I don't ever remember this much death in all the years I've lived in this town," said Dolores, shaking her head while reaching for a Kleenex.

"Nothing is like it used to be, Dolores. Nothing."

I walked out the door, got in the truck, and sat for a while. The last thing in the world I wanted to do was make that lonesome drive out to Hannah's place. I'd call Sam once I got out of town. I hoped that bitchy wife of his wouldn't answer the phone. I also worried about the women living there; they had no place to go. I assumed Sam and Leslie would inherit the place and put the girls out on the road as soon as they could. I needed to find housing for them, and that was not an easy thing to do in a community strapped for cash and with few resources.

I poked my head back in the door to remind Dolores to let Deputy Stancik know about the body in Junction. He'd need to confirm if it was Ava. I got back in the truck, slammed the door, and started the engine. Damn. My friend Hannah was gone. We'd never forget her in this town, especially me.

It took four rings for Nocona to answer his phone. He was probably with his gal pal in Del Rio.

"I need you to meet me at Hannah's. I'm on the road now. Think we got a positive on Ava. Stancik is going there now to ID the body in Junction."

"I tried to track her, sheriff, but the storm stopped that. Don't know what's worse, drowning or Lee Chapman, but it's over for her. I'll be at Hannah's right away."

I hung up and dialed Sam's number. He picked up on the first ring.

"Ronnie, haven't heard from you in a while. How's it going?"

"Sam, I'm afraid I have some bad news. Your mother passed away last night. She appears to have fallen while taking a walk. I'm going out there now."

It was quiet for a few moments, but I could hear him clearing his throat, then catching his breath a time or two.

“What was she doing out in that storm? Is one of the girls from the shelter involved in this?” He wasted no time in coming back with his self-righteous, accusing anger. But I understood it. I’d never seen that man cry, even when he was a snot-nosed brat growing up. As the only child of a rich, older man and devoted mother, Sam was an entitled mama’s boy.

“I don’t think so, Sam. I talked to Liz this morning. She and her husband are out there now. Looks like your mother took a walk with her dog before the storm hit full force. She might have tripped while out there and hit her head.”

“Ronnie, you need to button up that house and property. We don’t want people walking around and hanging out in our house. Leslie and I are on our way.” Sam hung up without another word.

I pulled off to the side of the road and reached for my Tums bottle in the console. I ate four of them, thinking about Mr. and Mrs. Sam Durand.

CHAPTER EIGHTEEN

Nocona Ketemoczy
Rocksprings, Texas

I dreamt of Jo last night. We were swimming in the South Llano River. She was laughing and doing handstands in the water. It was a beautiful sight, those bare legs high in the air, her red hair coiled, floating on the water's surface. We had left our clothes on a pile of rocks by the river's edge. There was no one for miles around.

After swimming, we walked hand in hand to a clump of switchgrass near a pecan tree. We made love, then I cupped my body against hers until we both fell asleep. A chilling breeze off the river woke us up near dusk.

Within that dream, I dreamt of my great-great-grandfather, the Comanche chief. It was as if the image of Jo's coiled hair became a snake, raveling itself into a tight circle. The snake's rattle sounded, then it moved from its circle form and became a hawk flying directly over me. The vision continued as the hawk landed at my feet and became my grandfather. He pointed to an area a yard or so away. I followed him as he guided me on a journey, revealing images and information buried deep within my subconscious.

My grandfather and I traveled through time to Fredericksburg, Texas, 1847. He transformed into the young Penateka Comanche chief he once was. He stood next to Buffalo Hump and the other chiefs. They were joined by John Meusebach and the immigrant Germans who came to Texas as part of the Fisher-Miller Land Grant.

That land grant was nearly four million acres between the Llano River and the Colorado River. It was the heart of Comancheria, the hunting grounds of The People.

There was much celebration between the Germans and Comanche as they gathered to sign the peace treaty between the Old and New Worlds. The treaty allowed the German settlers to move freely in Comanche territory without fear while also allowing the Indians to move freely within the White settlements. Indians were paid for the survey of their lands. A vision of peace and prosperity for the Germans and Comanche was sealed by the smoking of the Calumet by both parties.

Grandfather kept repeating, "El Sol Colorado, the red sun." It was the name he had given John Meusebach because of his reddish-blond hair. I then had a vision of Jo's reddish-blond hair coiled on the surface of the South Llano River. Again, the present and the past merged.

Grandfather then looked directly at me, so close to my face that our noises touched. Through his eyes, I saw Jo in a dark space. I saw chains wrapped around her neck. Then I saw Hannah, lifeless near an oak tree. My grandfather spoke. "Nocona. Prepare for the battle to come." He showed me his knife with its handle made from a piece of deer antler. He raised it high in the air above his head and cried to the Blood

Moon above him. The earth and sky merged as one, then the dream ended. It left me with a rush of electricity coursing through my veins, my heart pounding in my chest. With sweat-soaked sheets, I eventually passed out.

I was awakened by the ringing cell phone next to the bed. The sheriff confirmed my dream of Hannah, but where was Jo?

I sent her a text.

I'm sorry I haven't been in touch. Working too much. No excuse. I have to see you, Jo.

I got dressed and drove out to Casa de Katia. An ambulance and several trucks were parked in front, including the sheriff's truck.

The sheriff met me on the front porch.

"I'm glad you got here before Hannah's son and daughter-in-law. All hell's about to break loose."

The storm hadn't caused much damage at the ranch except for a few tree branches near the front porch. I looked over at the corral and saw some of the girls. They were talking and looking back at me and the sheriff. It was a cold and somber morning.

"Hard to image Hannah having a difficult son."

"They're quite the couple, Sam and Leslie. Leslie has been pulling the nose ring on her husband since day one."

"I guess they want the house and land."

"Yep. When the body gets cold, the money gets hot."

The EMTs were carrying Hannah, completely covered on the gurney, into the ambulance. I heard the girls cry out from the corral.

"It's a sad day for a lot of people. Come on, Nocona. Let's take a walk."

I followed the sheriff back behind the house quite a distance until we came to an oak tree near a large limestone rock jutting up from the dirt. As I got closer to it, I saw blood.

"Don't mess with the scene. Sorry, I'm so used to working with the deputy. I apologize. You know what's going on here," the sheriff said.

I walked to the oak tree and stood in its shade. Jack, Hannah's dog, was lying underneath it.

"Jack. Good dog," I said, rubbing his head.

He didn't get up but stayed beneath the tree, looking toward the limestone rock where his mistress once lay. I sat by him and looked closely at the tree. I could see the deer were in velvet because the bark was stripped in places. I followed the raw bark from the lowest branch to the trunk. There were markings on the tree. At the trunk, there was scarring from something tied several times around it. It might have been done by the Comanche, who used yucca as rope. The old oak was probably one of their marking trees. The Comanche would use marked trees to guide each other in Comancheria. I took a deep breath, thinking of the original owners of this land, The People, my people. And I thought again of the cruel story repeated throughout history of the owners of the land and the conquerors of the land.

Some called the trees target trees. Whatever name the historians used didn't matter. I was sitting beneath a sacred tree of the Comanche, a few feet from where Hannah took her last breath. And I knew without a doubt that my fate was closing in on itself as I completed the journey from its very beginning at the Mercado de las Brujas in Mexico City.

The sheriff approached Jack and me with a tight face, trying to hide his grief for Hannah and the crushing responsibilities of his job.

"I need to get back to the office. Come on and walk with me, Nocona. Dolores has been burning up my phone since we've been out here. Sounds like Harold Brune is stirred up. Said he saw wild hogs eating a fawn in broad daylight. Poor old man called it an omen and wanted to warn Hannah, but he couldn't reach her on the phone."

"That's a tough one, Ronnie," I said, standing up. "You think Jack will follow us back to the house?"

"The girls have been trying to get that dog back all morning. Jack's not leaving until he gets hungry, then he'll eat and return to this exact spot. Not the first time I've seen dogs holding vigils at their owners' graves. Humans don't even come close to that kind of unconditional love."

CHAPTER NINETEEN

Leslie Durand
Casa de Katia

It took all of five minutes to clear the riffraff from the house. Something I've wanted to do since Hannah started this crazy nonprofit, eating up our inheritance and causing sleepless nights for Sam. We've spent the past few years waiting for that phone call, announcing my mother-in-law's kidnapping or murder by a trafficker. At least the old woman died on the land she loved, instead of in a nursing home. I guess that was the blessing in all this mess.

When we arrived, Sam made a beeline to the sheriff. I took the opportunity to go in the house and assess the damage. I was surprised Elizabeth Gonzales wasn't here. She was hired to be Hannah's second in command. Instead of Elizabeth, some mousy blonde was sitting in the kitchen drinking a cup of coffee.

"And who are you, sitting in here like you own the place?"

"I'm Megan, ma'am. I work here."

"Well, Megan. Things are about to change. I doubt you'll keep this job and your free room and board much longer."

"Ma'am, are you Sam's wife? Ms. Hannah's daughter-in-law?"

"Yes, I am. Now get back to the bunkhouse until you hear from me and Sam."

The little mouse squeaked a gasp, then pleaded, "But what do I tell the other girls who live here?"

"Tell them to start packing."

Then the little mouse proceeded to cry her eyes out.

"If there's going to be any weeping and gnashing of teeth around here, it will be done by my husband and children, grieving for their mother and grandmother. I have no empathy for those living high off the hog, rent free. Now button it up."

And away the mouse scampered.

"What's going on, Leslie? Who's the girl? Sam asked as he walked into the kitchen with Sheriff Hoffman up his butt.

"I'm cleaning house, Sam. Something your mother should have done a long time ago. Maybe she'd still be here if she hadn't let strangers move in."

Sam hung his head low just like he always did when emotional truths were too much for him to bear. It took very little for him to go there, especially the older he got. Thirty-five years of living with an emotionally crippled man, and you quickly become an expert on reading body language.

"Now hold on a minute, Leslie. I'll find a place for these women, I assure you. There's no need to threaten them with being homeless."

"It's not a threat, sheriff. And you are way out of line making this your business."

"Are you sure this house belongs to you and Sam? Sam, did your mama name you power of attorney in the will? If so, you've got a copy of the will, and we can get this settled."

"How dare you, sheriff!"

"Leslie, it is my business as a board member of Casa de Katia. Hannah and the board discussed the possibility of her death and what would happen to the girls and the organization. I don't know what's in her will. But you and Sam need to find out before you throw those women out."

"Sam, I'm sure your mother designated you power of attorney."

"No, I'm not, Leslie. I don't have a copy of the will. She never spoke to me about it. I just assumed we'd inherit everything."

"Sam! Assuming makes an ass out of you and me!"

I swear to God I could have strangled both of those men with my bare hands. With no one running this shit show, I'd have to do it.

"Sam, get your mom's lawyer on the phone. We want to meet with him now."

"Leslie, first I'd like to call the local priest and set up the funeral arrangements with the church."

"Well, that will take all of five minutes. Call the lawyer," I demanded.

"Sam, once you get a day and time for the services, let me know. I'll notify the local paper. We'll make sure the funeral notices are placed at the grocery store, gas stations, and restaurants in town," the sheriff offered. "This town loved her. They'll want to be at the service."

"Sheriff, once more, mind your own damn business. You're not a member of this family," I said, motioning him with my hand to get out. "Take that border agent with you. He doesn't need to be wandering around out here."

"Sam, I'll give you a call later," the sheriff said, placing his hat on his head. "Leslie, good to know you haven't changed a bit over the years."

His smart-ass remark went unregistered. People no longer hurt my feelings with what they said and did. I stopped caring about what others thought of me a long time ago. I ignored the sheriff's glare and sat at the kitchen table with Sam.

"Honey, I know this is a hard time for you. Let me carry the heavy load. Call the priest, but give me the number for the attorney. I'll set up an appointment for us this afternoon."

"Leslie, we haven't even called the boys. Will and Aaron loved their grandma. Especially Will."

I squeeze his hand for reassurance, but what I was truly thinking about was when I buried my mother, Crazy Connie. She was the queen of the paycheck daddies and the life of the party. God rest her soul, if you could find it.

There was no designated grieving time for me when my mother died. I had grieved all my life having Connie as my mother. No one offered to bury her or read a eulogy because she was a train wreck. I simply called a funeral home, gave them a credit card number, and had her cremated.

I did it all by myself, just like I did it all by myself when I was a kid. I stole her checkbook and wrote hot checks at H-E-B when there was nothing to eat. I cleaned the house and woke her up for work when she had a job. For the seventeen years I lived with Connie, I took care of her.

There was no sitting around, wringing my hands, woe was me during those days. No seawall was built by my mother to protect me from the realities of life. I learned early on how to survive. It made me absolutely despise self-indulgence in others, with their grieving and weeping. I gave my sympathy to Sam because he was a good provider. The man loved me, and I loved him the best I could, despite growing up with Crazy Connie. When it came to my boys, my love and focus were there the minute they came into this hard world. I lived and breathed for my boys, so they'd never know the hurt I knew as a kid.

Once our sons and the local priest were notified, I made an appointment with Hannah's lawyer, Frank Adler, in Rocksprings. By three p.m. we were sitting in Adler's cracked leather chairs in front of his beat-up desk.

"Good to see you, Sam, Leslie. I'm sad to hear of Hannah's passing. She was a good woman and loved by many."

"Thank you, Mr. Adler. They'll be a funeral Mass at St. Mary's Saturday at 10," Sam said with his head beginning to hang.

Here we go, I thought to myself. Sam was already falling apart.

"Mr. Adler, we don't have a copy of the will. We're unsure of the ownership of the land and the house," I began. "There are women living in the bunkhouse, part of the Casa de Katia nonprofit Hannah started."

"Yes, I'm well aware of Hannah's generosity."

"If you'll let me finish, Mr. Adler. I'll get directly to the point. What's in that will?"

"Please, call me Frank. I am serving as power of attorney and the executor of Hannah's will. Sam, you were given the responsibility of medical power of attorney. However, with Hannah's unexpected death, that position is no longer necessary."

"How in the hell is that legal?" I demanded, as Sam's face nearly fell to his chest.

"It's quite legal, Leslie. Hannah didn't want to burden her son with settling the estate and any outstanding debt she had. I'll take care of all that."

"Frank, could we go over a simplified version of the will? We got some women living out at the ranch. We need to know. Leslie, please. Don't interrupt him," Sam said.

"Of course. Your mother left the house and the 640 acres to the Casa de Katia board. You are left with considerable stocks, cash, and other investments your parents made many years ago."

"Why does this not surprise me? Actually, it's better than I thought. The house hasn't been remodeled in sixty years. I stopped going out there years ago," I said, taking Sam's hand in mine. "Honey, it will be okay."

"My mother and father loved that place, Leslie. I was raised there. It should mean something to you, but I know it never did."

I stood up and hugged him. I had to get him out of there before he started crying.

"I understand, sweetheart. Frank, as the executor of Hannah's will, you need to notify the Casa de Katia board members immediately. We don't want to talk to them or deal with the women living out there. I doubt there's anything in that house that I want, much less my boys. I'm sure Sam feels the same. We're going back to San Antonio until the funeral."

I took Sam's hand and led him out of that law office. In three hours, we'd be back in the quiet calm of Alamo Heights, the walled city within San Antonio. I liked my big house and neighbors. I particularly liked how money separated us from the masses and their messy lives. I earned that wide berth of separation by surviving my childhood and being smart enough to marry a man like Sam.

CHAPTER TWENTY

Nocona Ketemoczy
Rocksprings, Texas

I followed the sheriff's truck back into town after we left Hannah's place. The sheriff was whipped. I couldn't blame the man after meeting Sam and Leslie Durand. That woman was a piece of work I refused to let get in my head.

I was on fire from my dream, thinking of Jo and wanting to drop Chapman. When the sheriff and I drove off, I looked at each girl's face, watching us leave. You could almost hear what they were thinking as they stood almost shoulder to shoulder in front of the bunkhouse. We were like all the other men they'd known in their short lives, full of empty promises one minute and driving away the next.

Ronnie and I had a bad track record on this case. Three girls were dead. Their only mistakes were taking one more dangerous chance in escaping one hellhole for another. Ava's desperation drove her to run in a blinding rainstorm along a swollen river, only to drown in that same river hours later. The senselessness of it ate my gut raw.

After the sheriff and I crossed the cattle guard at the ranch entrance, the sheriff pulled off to the side of the road. Joseph and Elizabeth Gonzales were approaching the entrance in a late-model Expedition. The sheriff walked over to the driver's side of the vehicle. I turned off my engine and got the window down, wondering if I should approach them. These people had known each other for years. Hannah's death was a tremendous loss for them. I kept my distance out of respect although I could hear every word they said.

"Joseph. Liz. Are you here to take care of the girls?"

"Good morning, Ronnie. We drove out to help sort things through. Got a call from Frank Adler earlier. You might remember him from our board discussions in the past," Liz stopped talking and looked in my direction. I nodded at her. "Hannah left the ranch to Casa de Katia, Ronnie. We're driving in to let the girls know they have a home. We'll check the supplies for the girls and the animals. I'm staying in the bunkhouse for a few days until things settle down. Ava and Hannah are gone. It's just too much for all of us."

Joseph looked at his wife then reached across the car seat to place his hand protectively on her right shoulder.

"Sheriff, we're not going into that house until after the funeral. By then, Sam and Leslie should be long gone to San Antonio. Adler said there'd be no need for them to come back out here. The furniture, all the household goods are left to the nonprofit," Joseph said, looking over at me.

"Sure takes a load off my mind to hear this," said the sheriff. "Let me know if you need anything from me or the department."

Liz started the Expedition. "I'm grateful we can get on with the work we do out here. I'll let you know when we meet as a board. Hopefully soon. We have a lot to do. Mr. Adler can address the specifics of Hannah's will at that time."

The sheriff leaned forward into the interior of the cab to shake hands with Liz and her husband, then he walked back to his truck. Before getting in the cab, he turned and looked at me.

"Partner, I feel like I can breathe again, hearing the good news about Hannah's will. Let's stop when we get to town and grab a bite to eat. I need to recharge."

I agreed and followed him into Rocksprings. Knowing that the girls at the ranch would be well taken care of helped ease some of the worry, but I still hadn't heard from Jo. No text, nothing. I wasn't quite ready to bring the sheriff in on all this. Being in separate vehicles gave me the chance to make a quick call in private. The first call was to the Del Rio border agent station to find out if she made it to work. She had to answer her desk phone, regardless of who the caller was on the other end.

"Agent McKenney, please."

"She's out. Want to leave a message?"

"No message."

No news was bad news. I knew I had to tell Ronnie what was up. It was getting deeper by the minute. My anxiety continued with my head spinning the dreams of Jo and my grandfather. It all pointed to one conclusion. Jo was surveilling Chapman at his ranch. Alone.

It was my fault for neglecting her. It didn't matter that I followed Ava. It didn't matter that I helped Ronnie out at Hannah's. The only thing that mattered was my piss-poor communication with her. I let her down. Something she never did in Afghanistan when I needed her.

I stared at the road in front of me, noticing the sheriff's slight turn onto North State Street then into the parking lot of the Kingburger. I parked the truck and followed the sheriff through the front door.

"Is Danny cooking today?"

The sheriff's loud mouth had everyone in the place looking at us.

"If Dan the man is here, I'm having Loco Moco."

The same tired waitress was there, looking at both of us.

"Sheriff, you and your friend have a seat. We won't let you go hungry. Over here, hon.

There's a clean table," she said, pointing to the lone empty table in the place.

He laughed out loud, in a celebratory mood because the girls were safe back at the ranch.

He had no clue as to the shit that was about to hit the fan. He shook hands at the tables of locals, asking about the weather and how everyone had made out in the storm. To lighten the mood, he quickly switched to talk of Friday night's anticipated football game. He was shooting the breeze like a bigshot in town without a care in the world. He showed no embarrassment nor recognized the simple fact he interrupted everyone in the place with his grand entrance and one-sided conversations.

We sat down, and I could tell by the look on his face he wanted me to ask him what Loco Moco was. I'd be damned if I would, like he was some culinary genius and had one up on me. I knew the classic Hawaiian meal quite well. It was the breakfast of champions for many hungover Marines: a bed of rice layered by a hamburger patty, two over-easy eggs, all covered in savory gravy. Because it took so long for your stomach to digest that amount of food, you were guaranteed a deep sleep for a couple of hours.

"Sheriff, I'm having coffee. Got a lot on my mind, and food is the least of it."

"I thought you'd be happy to know about the nonprofit running the ranch. The girls are safe. Not to mention that storm could have killed a lot more people than it did. We've had worse times with flash floods here."

"Lee Chapman is still out there, waiting for us to stop his killing spree. I think Jo might be taking care of that on her own."

"How do you know that?"

"She never reported to command what she found at the ranch outside Del Rio. We haven't spoken in two days. I called the Del Rio station today. She's out."

I wasn't about to tell him about my dreams. He already thought I was a nutcase with all the talk about unclean spirits and my relationship with a witch who'd been following me since I was a kid.

"Lovers' spat?"

I jumped from my chair and grabbed his throat. With all heads in the place turned in our direction, the sheriff pulled my hands off his throat.

"Settle down," he whispered to me. "I'm a good guy."

I sat down, embarrassed by my lack of control.

"I apologize. No excuse. Maybe lack of sleep and guilt. I knew Jo was going out there alone. I failed to launch a defensive. I put her in harm's way, Ronnie."

"Let's go." The sheriff stood up and placed a twenty and a ten on the table.

"You got my six, sheriff?"

"You bet!"

When we were out in the parking lot, I stopped him.

"Follow me to my apartment and wait. I got to pick something up before we drive out there."

She was standing by my door dressed in the traditional costume of *Día de los Muertos*, a ring of flowers around her skull, white faced with blackened eyes and nose. Of course, it was The Day of the Dead, November 1. I felt like the past two days had lasted ten years. The Witch of Sonora was silent until I walked out of the apartment carrying the Bullseye, the knife my father gave me. She shrieked with laughter.

"Nocona, you are the same scared boy I met at the Mercado de las Brujas in Mexico City all those years ago. A little boy playing with a rubber knife."

"I'm sending you back to hell, witch."

I plunged the knife into her, only to realize it went completely through without hitting muscle, sinew, or organ. I stumbled forward when the force I exerted met nothing. Nothing was there—because she wasn't real. She was a manifestation of my people's genocide and the horrors I saw in Afghanistan. The shame and guilt I lived with day after day, year after year, sucking me dry until I was a shell of a man. I slid the knife into my right boot and walked away, knowing my time with her was coming to an end.

CHAPTER TWENTY-ONE

Lee Chapman
Ranch near Canyon Rim
Del Rio, Texas

"Home, home on the range." I loved singing as much as I loved planning a party. Got my heart pumping just thinkin' about what today would bring. El Día de los Muertos had arrived. I had my makeup on with white goo for my face and black goo for my eyes, mouth, and nose. My chickadees had picked me up a little makeup kit at the Family Dollar in town.

I was doing my own version of Day of the Dead, complete with firing up the cauldrons from the shed. There would be no remembering the dead but rather a celebration of making people dead for El Día de los Muertos. Step aside, nonbelievers, pastor was gonna preach today!

I had my little chickadees move one cauldron out onto a large slate of limestone, where the heat of the sun and the fire would burn white ash into the rock. I wanted to make our little border agent part of today's celebration by adding her to my bone collection.

"Chickadees, get the lard out or you'll end up in the cook pot."

It appeared Renata, slow as all get out, needed a reminder that slothful movement was a deadly sin. She needed a taste of that good ol'-time religion, Palo Mayombe, to quicken her pace. At least Krystal responded quickly to my orders. Her delivery might be sloppy as hell, but she got it done.

I poked Renata's back with the tip of an aoudad horn I kept for such emergencies. It pierced the skin, causing it to bleed. She wailed away.

"You know what you can do with those tears, don't you? You can file them in the hurt-feelings department." I laughed and threw the horn at her head, causing her to scamper closer to Krystal.

"Watch it, bitch." Krystal said, shoving Renata away.

"Now girls, fight nice. There's a lot of work to be done, and I need you both to pay close attention," I laughed.

I made a 360, surveying my kingdom, miles and miles of Texas with two young women running at the crack of my whip. Not bad for a Florida cracker who survived on three hots and a cot for years.

I couldn't rest on my laurels...no, siree, there was work to be done. I needed to chop up the little border agent and get her in the cook pot. Numero uno on today's agenda. I walked toward the shack to see if she was conscious.

"Miss Border Agent, time to rise and shine. Oh, still asleep? Well, you should have left that Do Not Disturb sign on the doorknob."

I gave a whack to her left knee with my trusty hammer. That seemed to do the trick. She was wide awake now, howling like a banshee.

"Me and the girls will be moving you to one of our shipping containers today. I've got all kinds of toys in there...dental chairs, cattle prods, power tools out the ying yang."

She began thrashing around, well, what little she could in the chains wrapped around her.

"You were a busybody and got into those shipping containers, didn't you? I know you were in my shed, looking at my special skull collection. You were on private property, missy. You should have known better. You didn't bother to ask, just waltzed on in like you owned the place."

I gave the other knee a whack to make the pain even steven.

"Now, take your punishment like a good girl and promise never to do it again. Here in Texas, people don't put up with trespassers. Now, on to the business of the day. Day of the Dead, that is, a day of retribution."

She was out like a light. I slammed the door shut for good measure and walked back toward the ranch house. I needed some protein before I got down to business. Then I saw it. A small glint of light out of the east, near the ridge. I grabbed my binoculars off of the patio table and looked again.

Sure enough. Some old dude was locked into position a few feet away from a border agent in uniform. The agent had a .308 M14 rifle with a Leupold Mark 5HD scope. The sun reflected off his scope, making small glints of light. The old guy had a Colt AR-15.

"Bring it," I shouted to their location. "I got my own Gucci bag, boys. A M249 SAW firing up to 850 bullets a minute. I ain't no thickheaded drug runner. You've got the right-hand man of El Jefe in your sight. Big men carry big guns, idjits."

I laughed to myself, walking into the house, eating two Slim Jim beef sticks to get my hyperglycemia down. A second later, my headache was gone, and I wasn't shaky. Confusion and recklessness were not invited to the party. Even though it was basically three against two, my handicap was the slower-than-Christmas Renata and the dumbass Krystal. Then I stopped in my tracks. I got it. They came for the girl. The border agent in the shed. I laughed even harder. The boys wanted to rescue the girl, the biggest testosterone charge in the world. Talk about dumbasses. Those dudes would end up like all heroes, dead.

I grabbed another Slim Jim and walked back out to where the chickadees were carrying boxes of firestarter logs for the cauldron. Cheap and effective, those fire logs.

"Chickadees, we'll need more cauldrons. We have guests for dinner. That means more chickens in the pot, chickens in the pot, chickens in the pot!"

CHAPTER TWENTY-TWO

Nocona Ketemoczy
Ranch near Canyon Rim
Del Rio, Texas

The Rio Grande glistened behind me in the morning sun. The irony of its natural beauty in contrast to it being one of the world's largest trafficking corridors wasn't lost on me. For centuries people, animals, and contraband have crossed the river from one world to another. The Mexicans called it Rio Bravo. The Navajo called it Tó Ba'áadi. The Comanche routinely crossed it into Mexico on horse raids in the nineteenth century. Today it was the twenty-first century's River Styx, a border between the underworld and the world of the living. It could change a life or end it.

It was easy finding Chapman's ranch from the descriptions Jo gave me in our last conversation. I found her Jeep not far from a dirt road near a steep ridge overlooking the ranch. The sheriff and I traced her footprints up the ridge. Once there, we traced where her body had been dragged from a group of boulders she must have positioned herself behind.

Ronnie and I found a few mesquite trees and creosote bushes that gave us some cover while providing a panoramic view of Chapman's domain. We watched two skinny girls drag a cauldron onto a large slab of limestone several yards from the ranch house and a tin-roofed shed.

"What the hell?" the sheriff whispered to me.

"Yeah. Part of the Palo Mayombe circus act."

"No kidding, Nocona. I'm the one who told you about it, remember? I just didn't think I'd ever see a cauldron up close."

"Let's make sure none of them hear or see us. I'm splitting us up and moving to that piñon pine a few yards to your right."

I didn't think the tree would provide much cover since it was rooted in rock and twisted at a strange angle by the wind, but I had to get away from him and all the talking. I took the knife out of my boot and shifted my weight before walking over.

"You got a tomahawk in the other boot?"

"Shut up. Man, just shut your stupid mouth."

"Dial it down or you'll get us both killed, partner. I know you're crazy about the girl, but patience is the name of this game."

"Come on, sheriff. Let it go. You're not my boss."

"Just trying to keep us alive."

I walked away from him and crouched beneath the piñon tree, trying to bring my heart rate down. My hands were trembling. I steadied myself by watching a hawk flying above me, in and out of the sun's rays. Then I heard a man's voice. I picked up the binos and saw Chapman looking in my direction. He was nothing but a deranged animal howling into the canyon. His face was covered in the Catrina makeup like the skeletons masquerading during the Day of the Dead. I signaled to the sheriff. Chapman knew we were here.

I looked up at the hawk still circling above and heard her voice when the wind pushed underneath the hawk's wings.

"Nocona, your entire life has led you to this day. You are stronger than you know. You are the direct descendant of a Comanche chief."

Hannah. I knew she was with me, just as I knew I'd soon encounter Chapman. The juxtaposition of the two human beings, good and evil, was like a lightning bolt piercing my soul. I crouched low to the ground and slowly made my way to Ronnie. I was ready to end Chapman's killing spree.

"I'm going in. Once the fireworks start, get down there."

He nodded. I made my descent into hell, scrambling down the ridge with rocks sliding beneath each step I took. I stopped behind a large silver yucca and viewed the fire beneath the black cauldron. Chapman and the two girls were carrying Jo toward the white heat radiating from the limestone it rested on. Wondering who the girls were, I picked up the binos and saw the trademark Palo Mayombe tattoo of a cauldron and bones inked on their necks.

Chapman removed the chains from Jo's neck and waist then laid her spread-eagle in a circle made from the ash of former cauldron fires. The two girls tied Jo's hands and feet to wooden stakes. I was praying Jo was completely out and couldn't see the insanity before her. I looked toward the sheriff. He lifted his right hand to show he understood. Now was the time.

I descended another 150 yards, squatted in the rocks and sand, and viewed the madman through the rifle's scoop. He held a meat cleaver in one hand with an automatic weapon, belt fed, slung across his right shoulder. He made mistakes one and two in a heartbeat. He was in range and out of position to respond. I wanted to blow his head off but aimed for the left shoulder. I needed to keep him alive so I could question him later with the hope of exposing the entire drug-trafficking ring. I pulled the trigger, and a splattering of blood flew from his left side. The girls ran for cover behind the tin-roofed shed.

Chapman reached for his shoulder then crouched into position to return fire. Before he pulled the trigger, I heard a round of shots from the sheriff. The two girls ran from the shed to the ranch house. Chapman responded with a hail of bullets in the sheriff's direction. After that, nothing came from Ronnie. When I looked with the binos, he was on the ground.

"Come and get me. Hide and seek. Finders, keepers, losers, weepers," screamed Chapman. "But just a taste before I leave."

The bastard took the cleaver and walked toward Jo. Adrenaline pumped red hot through my veins, overtaking my senses. I found Chapman's temple in the rifle's scope and pulled the trigger. I took my knife out of my boot, the knife my father had given me, and ran toward him so I could finish the job.

He was still breathing when I placed the blade against his hairline. I grabbed his hair with my left hand to make it taunt, then pushed the blade across the top of his head. When I lifted his scalp from his head, a noxious vapor rose. The unclean spirit of the witch and the violence I knew as a Marine dispersed into the warm air of the canyon. And like my people, the Comanche who scalped their enemies, I did the same. I stood and faced the open sky above me, raising my arms with Chapman's scalp clenched in my right hand, crying out to the world my enemy was dead.

I then cut the rope from the stakes holding Jo. She was unconscious, and her breathing was shallow. Blood streamed from both knees. The chains around her had cut into her skin, causing bruising and bleeding. Her face and bare stomach were black and blue from where that piece of shit had kicked and beat her.

I stood up and called for Ronnie.

"Are you there? Can you move, Ronnie?"

"He about blew my damn hand off. I think I can walk though."

"Get the truck down here."

"Roger. What about those girls?"

"Later. Let's get you and Jo to the hospital."

CHAPTER TWENTY-THREE

Ronnie Hoffman
Val Verde Regional Medical Center
Level IV Trauma Emergency Department
Del Rio, Texas

The full moon brought the crazies out the past few days, making the ER tapped out with patients on gurneys in the hallway, waiting to be wheeled in for surgery or a recovery room. I was bleeding like a stuck pig despite the bandages and holding my hand in the air. I was still conscious, thank God, and hooked to an IV drip that delivered a nice cocktail of pain-free living. I looked over at Nocona and Jo. She was still out with machines and wires running all over her limp body. Nocona hovered over her, guilt written all over his haggard face.

I wondered if she'd be able to walk again. That freak did a number on her knees. She folded like a paper accordion when Nocona lifted her in the truck at the ranch. He sat with her in the back while I drove us to the hospital with my bleeding hand out the window, leaving a trail of blood from the firestorm we were lucky to survive. I kept thinking about the two girls who ran from the cauldrons toward the ranch house. I had a sick feeling in my stomach the nightmare wasn't over just because Chapman was dead.

I should have just wrapped my busted hand up and chased them down until I had them in handcuffs. Nocona would have gotten Jo to the ER without any trouble. I broke a golden rule I've had for myself since I was twelve years old in BSA Troop 207 of Edwards County. "Leave no trace," Scout Master Hahn drilled into us. In another words, leaving your garbage behind for others to clean up was a bad thing to do. There was no way I'd be able to rest until I found those two girls who worked for Chapman.

I stared at Jo on the gurney, willing her to health. Nocona was already wired with guilt and revenge before we even showed up at the ranch. Looking at him hanging over the gurney, I saw the nerves in his neck and eyes twitching into overdrive. He took it personally for everything and everyone that went down in this case. Then there was all the bullshit with the witch feeding on his pain. The entire case was a freak show from the start.

It wasn't helping that I was within earshot of the ER. I could hear every scream, from a kid who cut his foot open on a piece of glass to a little girl who broke her arm falling off her bike. There were moaners in there who insisted the gun fired on its own. There was typically no foul play involved in those cases, just another idiot who had a gun and no clue how the damn thing worked. I sighed and reminded myself I should have stayed at Chapman's ranch and followed the two girls who got away. My time would have been better spent than in this place.

Two orderlies finally showed to wheel Jo into surgery. Nocona stood up to follow them but was stopped by the simple hand wave of the male orderly. The anxiety gushed from Nocona's body with a force of air from his mouth. He collapsed next to me in a metal folding chair and went back to gnawing his right thumb.

"You need to quit biting yourself, buddy. You're making me a nervous wreck just watching you pull at your skin."

"Yeah. Bad habit I picked up as a kid. Kept me from smoking, I guess."

"Well, you're doing a real number on yourself, inside and out. It's hard to watch with this damn bullet still in my hand, thinking about you, Jo, my wife, and the two girls we let get away. You need to get up and make some phone calls, Nocona."

"You're right. Better than sitting here waiting."

"Call Dolores at the station. She'll let my wife know, and alert Jo's station in Del Rio. I imagine we're gonna get some kickback from those guys for not counting them in. We've made quite a list for the cleanup crew, Nocona. Feel exhausted thinking about all the work ahead. Hey, when you make your calls, see if you can find some cheeseballs for me. Might be some in the cafeteria. Doubt if they got 'em in vending machines, but you should check that first. May be an off brand, but I don't care."

"No, I'm not picking up any cheeseballs, sheriff, but I will call Dolores," he said, walking away from me.

I felt like an old man. I've been shot before in the line of duty, but I sure don't remember feeling this tired. My belly was bloated, poking through the thin hospital gown, and the sheets were full of blood on my left side. This was for the birds.

I should be on a tropical vacation with Mary. I'd been promising her a cruise since our tenth anniversary. It still hadn't happened. That damn Chapman could have blown my head off or crippled me. Life had always turned on a dime for me. I wasn't waiting to see what the fates would have in store for me at sixty-seven. High blood pressure and chronic indigestion were my daily companions. I'd have to kick the cheeseball habit like I did the smoking. Damn food snob, Nocona. He could have said it in a nicer way. Unpredictable man. You never knew what he'd say or do. Now, I was worrying again.

I had to concentrate on Mary and the family now. Once I was out of this monkey suit, I was cashing in the chips. Adios, Edwards County Sheriff's Department. I was sick to death of death and dying. I just couldn't make it any simpler than that.

"Dolores will call your wife," Nocona said, sitting back in the chair next to me.

"Appreciate it. I need to ask you something, and I want you to be straight with me. I been thinking about it since we got here, but with Jo in such bad shape I hated to bring it up. "

"Yeah?"

"I saw you take Chapman's scalp. Granted, I was bleeding and half out of my mind, but it was a clear view from where I watched. Damn, Nocona. I don't know what to say."

"There's nothing to say, sheriff. It happened, and Chapman is dead. End of conversation."

"What are we going to tell forensics? Don't you think we should have the same story?"

"Coyotes gnawed on Lee Chapman, sheriff. There's nothing to tell."

"Damn."

"Why don't you enjoy the drugs they're giving you and relax. I'll file the paperwork with my agency. You do the same for yours. Nobody cared about Chapman. He finally isn't anybody's problem. Taking his last breath was the best thing he ever did with his sorry life."

"What about the girls that were with him?"

"I called their descriptions in," Nocona said, turning around to watch two orderlies approach my gurney. One grabbed the IV pole, and the other began pushing the gurney down the hallway. "I'll walk down with you as far as I can."

"Jo is going to be okay, Nocona. You got her just in time."

"I hope so. I'm really counting on the miracles ortho surgeons can perform these days. A lot of my buddies got new limbs after they were blown off in Afghanistan. I thought about taking her to Brooke Army Medical in San Antonio if this place can't help. My brother-in-law had both knees replaced there. He's back to running again."

Nocona stopped at the entrance to surgery and touched my head.

"See you in a few. Sleep like a baby, sheriff."

When I came to in a private room, Nocona was sitting in the chair next to me with my wife.

"Mary, darlin'. I'm sorry I cheated us out of so many years with this job," I said, my eyes full of tears. "I'm going to make it up to you, baby."

"Now, Ronnie. Those pain meds are making you a little emotional. Don't get yourself worked up."

Noco was sitting behind Mary, laughing his ass off.

"You old softie. I never knew you had it in you," he said, standing up.

"Life is short. Yesterday was a good reminder," I added.

"You'd be bored in a week if you retired. What about your crowd at Kingburger? Hard for me to imagine you without an audience. Much less playing dominoes and watching *Family Feud* to pass the time."

"Nocona, when you're in your late sixties, you start to think how much time you have left. You think about all the things you talked about but never did, like fly-fishing in the Keys, taking your girl on a cruise. Doesn't have to be big stuff that's worth doing. It's more about not letting life pass you by. Right now, I'm just reacting to it, instead of living it. I want the time back I wasted away. I could still be in surgery, man. I could have been shot through the head instead of a hand. Chapman would have won, won my time. You don't think about things like that until it's at your back door."

"I get it, sheriff. It's the bitterness I live with when I think of my dad. He said all the things you're saying, but he wouldn't stop working. He was worried about the money. A heart attack took him from me. I never got to fish with him again, though we said we were going to soon. Soon never comes. It's just a word people tell each other."

A nurse walked into the room, brushing Mary and Nocona aside to take my vitals and check the IV drip.

"You need to sleep, sheriff. Your friends can visit with you later." She said, waving Nocona and Mary toward the door.

"Mary, how about some lunch?" Nocona asked her after she bent down to kiss me goodbye.

"Don't be messing with my girl, Nocona. I'll have your scalp."

If looks could kill, Nocona would have followed through. I laughed out loud. I just couldn't help myself; I enjoyed pissing the man off.

"Ronnie!"

"Don't shush me, Mary. Nocona is a big boy. He can take it," I said, laughing again.

"The sheriff is going to take a nap now," said the nurse, turning off the light in the room and walking out with Nocona and Mary.

CHAPTER TWENTY-FOUR

Jo McKenney
Room 416
Val Verde Regional Medical Center
Del Rio, Texas

When I opened my eyes, I didn't know where I was. I followed the drainage tube snaking its way from my knees to a pump. The peripheral line supplied my drugs. Wires attached to my chest fed the vitals monitor. I had no idea how long I had been in a hospital. Panic struck as I forced my brain to recall my last memory.

On Halloween morning, I had sipped coffee, driving through the canyon, admiring the colors of the river and sky until I thought of Nocona. My mind was clouded. I made stupid mistakes every step of the way in my position to surveil Chapman's activities. I made myself vulnerable to a criminal. And like a vivid dream, the lost days came back to me. The pain. The thirst. The heavy chains. His knife reflecting the sun in my eyes. The airless heat of the shack. The gray alkaline dust in my eyes and mouth as the two girls dragged me through the rocks. My nostrils bleeding from the lack of moisture in the air.

I reached for my knees beneath the hospital sheet, hoping I still had use of my limbs. I felt the thickness of surgical tape, gauze, and material holding it all together. I remembered his hammer. The explosive blinding pain had soared through my body until I blacked out. What did that monster do to me when I was unconscious? How much of myself did I lose? I closed my eyes and let the tears fall, feeling small, a mean, pitiful low, wondering if he had raped me or cut me. I wanted my mom. I wanted her to tell me if I'd be able to walk again. *Mama, will I have the same life I had before?*

When I woke up again, a nurse was changing the IV bags.

"Good to see you awake, Josie."

"How long have I been here?"

"Two days, following surgery. The doctor will see you on his rounds today and fill you in on the prognosis. There's a lot of people who are anxious to see you. Your mom and dad are right outside the door, anxious to get in. A good-lookin' border agent has been here since the first day. Feel like having company?"

"Just my mother. No one else."

"Okay. Anything else I can get you? Liquid diet for a while. Drink your water." She reached for a large water bottle with a straw. "I'm going to hold it for you till you are steady. Let the straw do its job."

I took a small sip. It exhausted me, so I put my head back down on the pillow and stared at the yellow roses on the nightstand.

"From the border agent. He hasn't left the hospital since you've been here. He and a sheriff brought you in," the nurse said, returning the water bottle to the side table.

I made no reply. The words and the emotions I felt were

tied in a huge knot in my stomach and head. I closed my eyes again, hoping she'd leave.

When I woke up, my mother was sitting next to the bed. Sunshine Shelly was a special girl, raised in Rockport, Texas, to a shrimper father and a bookkeeping mom. She met my dad when he came to town one spring break, fishing for trout and pretty South Texas girls. Dad was from the high plains, old money, and SMU legacy. Shelly and Dennis were from different worlds, but they made it work. When I compared my life to theirs, I was a full-time resident in another galaxy, light years away from their world of goodwill and integrity. I wish their world and all its honest, unassuming rules for living still existed.

Their romance started at the Dairy Queen drive-through on Highway 35. Shelly had just started her shift after driving back from classes at Texas A&M-Kingsville. When she opened the little sliding glass door, Dad ordered a Hunger Buster, hold the mayo. Shelly took it upon herself to tell him he wasn't ordering correctly.

"Sir, I never met anyone in my life who ate a hamburger without mayo and mustard combined. I think you're making a big mistake. I'm going to fix it for you, so you can enjoy that hamburger."

Her confidence took his breath away, and the rest is history. Her only angst against her husband was his moving her to Dallas for a job forty years ago. She hated being north of I-10 in a land of "lying salesmen, pretentious women, and TV preachers."

Shelly lost her shine when she saw me now in the hospital. She looked old and worried to me. Her hair was cut too short, and she had stopped coloring it. Her hands were folded in her lap, and she stared at the bulge that were my legs underneath the white blanket and sheet. I could only image what I looked like to her.

I would give my poor mother the cruel job of telling me exactly how I looked in a minute or two, but what I really wanted her to do was lie beside me, cradle me in her arms, and sing the song she always sang when I was sad or hurt.

"Catch a fallen star and put it in your pocket, Jo-Jo. You can save it for a rainy day."

I so believed in my mom and that song that I spent my elementary years looking up in the sky for falling stars. I kept my pockets empty, waiting for my fair share.

"Mama."

She rose from the chair and stood next to me, putting my hand in hers.

"Josie, girl."

"I got hurt, Mama. Really bad. I should have listened to you a long time ago and returned to civilian life after Afghanistan. I thought I could do it, you know, be the boy Dad wanted, eat snakes, kill the bad guys. It was pride and stupidity that got me in this mess."

"Josie, honey. No, it wasn't your fault. It was just bad luck. Bad luck, that's all. You will get all this behind you, but it will take some time and a lot of rest."

"Oh, I got time, Mama. That's one thing I've always had was time alone."

"Josie. We're going to see you through this. I'm not going to leave your side. Neither is Daddy. Do you want to see him? He's right outside the door, waiting."

"I'm not ready to see anyone but you. I don't know if that man cut my face or raped me. You got to be brave and tell me. Tell me what you see, Mama. I need to know what my life will be like when I leave this place."

"There's plenty of time for that, Josie. You're alive. That's what matters. I'm not going to put you through an emotional upheaval now. Let's wait for the doctor. There's a lot of stuff we don't know yet," she said through tears. "Forgive me. Tears of a weak woman."

"Mama, give me the compact out of your purse."

"I don't have a compact in my purse, Jo."

"Don't lie to me. You've been carrying the same compact-and-lipstick combo for years. They're an extension of your hands when they aren't in your purse."

She turned away from me, sat down, and placed her purse on her lap. She wouldn't look at me as she opened the compact and cleaned the glass with a Kleenex from her purse. She stood up and placed it in my right hand.

I saw two black eyes, a split bottom lip and a torn upper lip. My eyebrows were burnt off, and part of my right earlobe was missing. My skin was bruised and cut where the chains had hung from my neck. They looked like angry, black welts.

"Let's see if he knocked my teeth out. My jaw is killing me despite the drugs."

I opened my mouth wide, and they were all there. I couldn't help but laugh.

"Mama, I still have my teeth! Can you believe it? He must have hit me a few times along the jawline, but I got my teeth. I have all my teeth, Mama!"

Sunshine Shelly laughed with me, then she stepped closer to my bed, rubbing my hands, massaging each finger, even each fingernail, split and broken. She hovered even closer until I felt each tear she cried slide from my forehead to my chin. Then I knew. I caught my fallen star the day I was born, and I kept it in my pocket all this time, calling it Sunshine Shelly.

CHAPTER TWENTY-FIVE

Nocona Ketemoczy
Val Verde Regional Medical Center
Del Rio, Texas

She didn't want to see me. I'd been standing guard outside her door for two days, watching her mother and father come in and out without acknowledgement or a word. I guess I should have introduced myself, but they both looked like hell. Jo's mother appeared a bit more stooped over every time she came out of her room. She was in there more than anyone else, including the hospital staff. I was glad Jo had a tight bond with her mom. A lot of women I've known in the military or even high school fought with their mothers. Seemed the mother was either jealous of her daughter's opportunities when comparing them to her own life or hated the attention the father doted on her daughter. There were few times in my life when I witnessed true unconditional love between a mother and a daughter. When I did, man, it was magic. It was also the best example of the mama bear thing, the rarity of unconditional love, which would make a mother do anything to protect her girl. I've met my share of mothers who wanted to kill me for the head games I played with their innocent daughters.

If a girl was on the verge of becoming a woman, the mother was the first to know. Those women protected their daughters' vulnerability with a death grip. They knew firsthand the heart-break of the approaching disaster of unrequited love. They smelled the fire and ran into the flames of adolescent love, unsuspected pregnancies, and dumping at the altar. I knew all about it. I was the SOB mothers hated. Manipulating women wasn't something I picked up from watching my father mistreat my mother. I had no one to blame. I was just lost for a long time in my own misery and couldn't care less how I spread it around. Military women rarely put up with that kind of shit, so I got older and wiser, as they say.

To think of mating for life like the sheriff and Mary blew me away. It was fantasy thinking for someone like me. The sheriff was already home and resting with his wife in Rock-springs. I never thought I'd miss him, but at least he was someone to talk to who knew the situation, every miserable piece of it, including a witch and a scalping. It was hard for me to find the humor in it like he did, but who knew what he actually believed about the situation? He kept worrying about the girls who got away. Man, I just couldn't add that to the list with Jo still here. I was consumed with her health and the hope she could forgive me.

Hoffman had reassured me more than once that I'd done my best at the ranch, and Jo would recover to a full and active life. Whether that life would include me was anyone's guess. Hoffman wasn't weighing in on that one. He wasn't a gambling man when it came to what women were capable of doing or saying. Forty years of marriage had taught him that, he said. The only advice he gave me was to let her talk and to keep my mouth shut when she was doing so.

I watched Jo's father leaning against the closed door frame of Room 416. He looked at me directly, popped his neck, and refocused his stare at the nurse's station. My vigil outside the door might have helped him put two and two together regarding me and Jo, but he never let on. I imagine every breath he took was centered on Jo's survival and comforting his wife. I felt bad for the couple for obvious reasons, but they were also in a strange land without family or friends for miles around. At least they had each other and the hope their only daughter would one day walk out of Room 416.

There wasn't any reason I should tell them who I was. I had no title, no claim to her. I was just another Marine she knew from her time in Afghanistan. Fast forward, I was just another border agent who happened to know her. None of it was the way I wanted it. Not by a mile. The only certainty I felt in any of this was I wasn't leaving this spot until she asked for me. And when she did, I wasn't leaving her side ever again.

"Nocona?"

Jo's mom stuck her head out of her daughter's room and called my name. My heart jumped through my chest, thinking her daughter wanted to see me.

Her father appeared and rushed to the door before I could say anything.

"What's going on, Shelly? Who in the hell is Nocona?"

"Sir, my name is Nocona. I served with your daughter in Afghanistan. I also brought her to this hospital several days ago."

"Dennis, Josie wants to see you, but she needs to talk to this young man first. Would you take me to get something to eat while they do? I could use some real coffee and a hot meal."

Jo's father nodded at me, and I extended my hand to shake

his. He shook my hand briefly then reached for his wife's arm. I watched them walk down the hospital corridor, holding hands, their heads slightly touching, inseparable in their movement.

I took a deep breath and realized I felt more awake than I'd ever felt in my life. Every nerve was twitching. Every heartbeat was in sync with my breathing. I had arrived at the turning point for the rest of my life. And it all depended on her.

CHAPTER TWENTY-SIX

Jo McKenney
Room 416
Val Verde Regional Medical Center
Del Rio, Texas

I heard him open the door, but I couldn't see him. The room was dark except for the light coming from a small opening in the drapes. He remained standing inside the room near the door. Maybe he was adjusting his eyes to the darkened room. No, he wasn't. Nocona was scared. He was afraid to see what I looked like, afraid to begin the heart-wrenching conversation of where we go from here. I wanted to laugh, thinking I had to be an improvement compared to the swollen, bloody face he saw at the ranch. But then I began to cry, thinking about the possibility he was here to say goodbye. I was on a steady diet of pain meds, so controlling my emotions was not going to be easy. Oh, what the hell, nothing was worth arguing at this point. We'd both seen each other at our worst. I wasn't going to pretend our relationship was based on friendship and shared history. I wasn't going back. *Noco, you'd better tell it like it is 'cause we're on the cliff; there's no more punting allowed.*

It was clear to me we had one choice to make that would determine the rest of our lives. We could either go our separate ways and never see each other again, or we could build a new life. I was done with Noco's fence-sitting. I nearly died at that ranch. There'd be no more wasting time for me. If Noco didn't want a life with me, fine. It would about kill me, but I'd eventually get over it. I could always move back home with my folks until I recovered.

All I wanted the man to tell was what I meant to him. It was what I deserved. And he knew it. That was the irony of it all. Noco was intuitive although he'd think that was a sign of weakness, relying on instinct instead of intel. What would it take for the grown man frozen in emotional fear to step toward my hospital bed and speak to me from the heart? I guess I'd have to lure him in with a bit of encouragement.

"Noco, is that you? Why don't you come in and tell me you're crazy about me, despite the shape I'm in," I said, making a faint attempt to laugh at the absurdity of his behavior.

"I'm here, Jo. Don't know how to do this."

"Do what?"

"Approach you, after everything that has happened. I don't know if you're going to curse me, maybe even slap me for never calling you back. You have that right. You also have the right to tell me to get the hell out of your life, after what happened to you at the ranch. I could have stopped it all with one phone call, but I never made the call. I got a piss-poor excuse that I was in a shit show on Halloween night. But that's no excuse. I let you down, Jo."

"Noco, can you come a little closer, so I can at least look at you?

His footsteps were deliberate and slow. When I felt him

standing next to the bed, I opened my eyes. His face. Oh, God, the guilt in his face about killed me.

"I know, Noco. I look a little rough, but you should see what the other guy looks like. Heard he was scalped before he took his last breath. You've always been handy with a knife, just like that time in Afghanistan with the goat," I said, laughing through my tears.

"Who told you that?"

"Ronnie Hoffman, the sheriff you've been working with, came to see me before he checked out. He said you were a one-man firestorm. Called you a hero."

"I don't deserve that."

He knelt down beside the bed and put his head face down into the sheets. I knew he was hiding his tears from me. I touched his head, weaving my fingers through his thick black hair. He reached for my hand and held it. We stayed like that for a long time, crying and holding each other.

I felt his body change position, so I opened my eyes, trying my best to sit up. He was still kneeling on the floor, but he was looking directly up at me. I could tell it wasn't easy for him, being that direct. His eyes were like those of a trapped animal, frantic and scared, begging me to unlock the cage. When he began to speak, his eyes welled up with tears.

"It's my fault you're in pain. I should have been there. I find it hard to forgive myself, let alone thinking you could ever forgive me. Damn near impossible to even imagine you could, but God, I want you to, Jo. We've covered a lot of ground together, especially in Afghanistan. That's the gut punch for me in letting you down. I'm a Marine, and I let you take the heat. I knew better. It was drilled in my head to leave no one behind. But I'm an arrogant man, thinking I had all the bases covered, that I'd get to you in time. Every excuse is just bull-shit. What do I need to do to change your mind about me? I'm capable of being a better man. Just tell me how to win you back."

"You don't need my forgiveness, Nocona. You saved me. I'm living and breathing right now because of you. And because of our work, Chapman is dead, six feet underground where he belongs. We removed a parasite from society. Mission accomplished. I feel damn proud of that."

He looked away from me as his eyes filled again.

"Don't hide those tears, Noco. I love you for them. You're a good man. But there is something you can do for me—forgive yourself for the past. And you know what I'm talking about. Afghanistan. That really bad day that somehow you thought you were responsible for. Like some demon was in your head calling you a murderer and you accepted the sentence. Walking around like a dead man, not allowing yourself to feel, just working to get through it all. Our night together opened the door to what we could be if you allowed yourself to be happy. Let me love you, Noco. Give me your heart. I gave you mine the night we made love."

"I've wanted to tell you how I felt about you for a long time, Jo. But my head hasn't been right for years. It started when I was a kid, being in a place I had no business being in. I know how crazy this sounds, but it's true. I opened the door to an evil spirit who about ate me alive, feeding on my insecurities and shame. Then Afghanistan happened. It was probably the nail in the coffin for me. I'm guilty as charged for the things I've done. I've also had a lot of depression about things in the past. I kept thinking a real man, a good Marine could take it. It wasn't until Hannah Durand, the widow who ran the safe house near Rocksprings, saw right through my bullshit. She prayed for me, made me believe I was connected to an honorable past, that I could cure myself if I could forgive myself. I broke the code of that pain when I saw you at Chapman's ranch. I went with my intuition and got you out of there. No second-guessing myself because I wanted you, Jo. You and Hannah, my dad, showed me how to love. And once I believed I was worthy of that, the evil in my head died. Please don't think I'm crazy."

That beautiful man climbed into my bed and wrapped his body around me.

"Careful with my knees, Noco."

He jumped out of the small bed quickly and hit his elbow on the IV pole, causing it to tip forward.

"I didn't hurt you, did I?" he asked, securing the IV pole in its place and pulling the sheets up to my neck. He reached over and placed a hand lightly on my left knee.

"No way, Noco. Now get back in this bed where you belong," I said, laughing.

CHAPTER TWENTY-SEVEN

A YEAR LATER

Nocona Ketemoczy
Kingburger
North State Street
Rocksprings, Texas

"You'd think the county would have enough money to give Hoffman a retirement party someplace other than Kingburger," I said to Jo, who had leaned her tripod cane with rubber stoppers against the truck. She then threw her jacket into the cab. She refused help every inch of the way of her recovery, regardless of pain and argument.

Our first arguments as husband and wife were always about me interfering with my "overzealous sense of responsibility." I kept trying to tell her that any decent husband would help his wife if he saw her struggling to walk. I'd see the sweat on her face, I'd hear the murmuring of curse words, and I flew into action. The woman was like a brick wall when it came to making a point about her need to do it on her own. She'd scream at me to get out of her way, while reminding me she'd never rebuild her muscles and stamina if she didn't do it the hard way.

Our trip to town was no exception as I watched the look on her face and the involuntary shaking of her right arm as she reached for the grab bar on the passenger side and hoisted herself up in the truck. Once inside, she reached for the cane outside the truck, pushing it near the door with her right foot until it was within arm's reach. She was about to fall out of the truck reaching for her cane, but I didn't say anything. I knew better.

"I thought you liked Kingburger. You're always bragging about the chicken-fried steak there, plus it's Halloween night. It's a festive occasion for two celebrations; otherwise, we'd be on the couch eating candy and staring at the TV," she said, short of breath from her efforts to get in the truck.

"Yeah, you're right. The food is good, and Hoffman loves the place. It's where I first met him. It's been almost a year to the day. Hell of a ride every inch of the way with him. That's why I didn't take him seriously when he got choked up about retirement and spending more time with Mary. I thought it was the pain meds talking. The man meant every word he said that day."

"We all chose better paths after Chapman's ranch, Noco. Best decision I made in my life."

I smiled at her, then started the thirty-minute drive into town. It had been a rapid-fire change in lifestyles since Jo checked out of the hospital. Within days, I carried her into the Justice of the Peace in Val Verde County for a civil wedding ceremony with her parents serving as witnesses. We had the reception at Molcajetes Restaurant, the same place that brought us good luck the last time we were there.

I asked the boss man for two weeks off to find a rental house for us outside of Rocksprings. I found one not far from

Hannah's. It was a three-two brick ranch from the seventies, on ten acres with a barn and a few big oaks. I knew once everything was cleaned up, it would make a quiet and safe place for Jo to recover.

I felt like a lucky man the day I signed the rental agreement and got the utilities turned on. Then I went into town and broke the lease on my crappy apartment. I didn't even wince when I lost the deposit. I spent a hell of a lot of money in those two weeks, but I was building a life for us with every step I took. I was singing along to Charlie Robinson on Texas Rebel Radio as I drove back to Del Rio to break Jo's lease and pack her stuff up, including the hammock and plants from the front porch. I knew it would make her happy to have them in our first home together.

Before I left town, I drove by Del Rio's animal services facility and adopted a dog to keep Jo company when I had to go to work. Cooper looked to be mostly Catahoula with his distinct coloring. He was nine years old and had hip issues.

"Once a dog is out of the cute-puppy stage, it gets harder and harder to adopt them out. Cooper is a sweet dog. Everyone here loves his temperament. He deserves a loving home," said the animal tech, bending down to pet Cooper. "You won't regret saying yes."

Cooper also came with a letter from his former owner who had to give him up to move into assisted living. It was apparent the old man loved his dog by the words he used to describe him, "loyal and protective, a true best friend." It was a real heartbreaker to think the man had few options for himself and his best friend at the last stage of life. Adopting Cooper was a no-brainer to me. I drove all the way back to our new home with Cooper riding shotgun.

The first months of Jo's recovery were hard for everyone. Her parents stayed for six weeks to help her adjust. Dennis was a big help, setting up the house and cleaning the barn behind it. Shelly kept us fed and drove Jo to PT when I worked.

"What you thinking about over there?" my wife asked me.

Yeah, that beautiful, sexy woman sitting next to me was my wife. Life was good.

"I was trying to remember if I put Hoffman's retirement gift in the truck."

She turned her head around to view the back seat.
"All there, a liter of Jamaican rum, two plastic leis, and two decorative cocktail glasses with straws. I say the sheriff and Mary are set for their tropical dream vacation."

"Don't be afraid to have a drink tonight, Jo. It wouldn't hurt to relax a little. You've been off the pain meds for a long time, so there's nothing to worry about. I'm your DD."

"No rum for me, but a Shiner would hit just right."

"Feels good being out, doesn't it, baby?"

When we pulled up to Kingburger, the parking lot was full and the music was blasting.

"I love this, Noco. I just love it," said Jo, reaching for her cane.

"Let me at least open the truck door for you, Jo. We can pretend it's a date."

"I guess you're expecting a goodnight kiss at the end of the evening with all this attention you're lavishing on me."

We both laughed.

Hoffman and his wife were standing by the open door, greeting everyone as they came in.

"Nocona! Good to see you and your better half," the sheriff said, offering his hand.

"So glad y'all could make it," Mary said, hugging both of us.

"What do you have in your hand?"

"Everything you and Mary need for a tropical vacation," I said. "Is there a gift table I can set this on?" I asked.

"Hand me that. I don't want anybody mistaking this for party fare tonight," said Hoffman.

"Nothing better than Myers's Rum, sheriff. I hope you and Mary enjoy it," said Jo. "We had a ball putting it together for you."

"Beauty and brains. You might want to think about running for sheriff, Jo, once you've fully recovered. The people of the county need you."

"That's quite the compliment, Ronnie. I'll think about it."

That was the last thing in the world I wanted for her, but it was Jo's call. Her eyes lit up the moment Hoffman mentioned the job.

"Ronnie will talk your head off, as you know," said Mary. "Y'all come on in and help yourself to brisket and the fixings. Beer and wine are next to the buffet table."

We ate until I heard the opening of the guitar chords for Robert Earle Keene's "Feeling Good Again." I loved the Texas songwriters. I could relate to every lyric they wrote. Couples were entering the makeshift dance floor near the center of the restaurant where the DJ had set up shop.

"You want to dance, Jo?"

"Absolutely. Do you mind if I stand on your toes and hold you tightly? I think I'd be able to balance myself without putting any strain on my knees if you can stand the pain."

"Holding you never hurt. Are you going to be able to let me lead? It'd be a hard thing to do for you, even while standing on my feet."

"Only this once, Noco. Only this once," she said, laughing, as I held her hand and walked her slowly to the dance floor.

"Now, jump on and don't let go, crazy girl."

After a few dances together, we ate and Jo had a few more

beers. The heavy food and beer had her falling asleep at the table.

"I'm carrying you out of here, bride."

"I'll let you. Between the beer and brisket, I'm done."

My wife sat next to me with her left hand on my thigh as I drove us home.

By the time I got the front door unlocked and let Cooper out, she was asleep in the cab. I carried her to bed, waking her up for a few minutes to undress her and put her nightgown over her head.

"Say goodnight, Jo."

"Goodnight, Jo." She was out when her head hit the pillow.

I walked outside for some fresh air, allowing Cooper to roam the property after being locked in the house most of the night. I was almost to the barn when I heard it, the sound of feet walking across the gravel road, leading to the house. Then I heard Cooper bark.

I followed the direction of the noise, stopping at the truck to get my Maglite and a pistol underneath the driver's seat. I checked to see if it was loaded, then I stuck it in the waist of my jeans and pulled my shirt over it.

The closer I walked to the sound of Cooper's barking, the more frantic it became. I no longer heard anyone walking the gravel road to the house. I shined the Maglite down the road in front of me and saw two figures looking down at Cooper. They immediately looked in the direction of the light when I was close enough, but I couldn't tell if they were male or female.

"Stop. Don't go any farther. You're on private property."

"We're lost," replied a female voice. "We're looking for Casa de Katia. We need help."

I was about a yard from them and could see both were females. Cooper continued barking and snarling at them. I wasn't calling him off. I reached for the pistol tucked in my waistband, removed the safety lock, and pointed it in the direction of the light. I wanted them to see that, so they realized there'd be no game-playing. Both were carrying backpacks. Who knew what was in them. After the hell we all went through at Casa de Katia, I wasn't taking any chances. The irony of it being Halloween night, exactly a year later, wasn't lost on me.

"We've been trafficked. Left to die out here. Don't point your gun at us," said the same female voice that had spoken before.

Now that they were within a few feet of sight, I could make out the cauldron-and-bones tattoo of Palo Mayombe on their necks. It was Krystal and Renata from Chapman's ranch. I spent a year tracking them to tie up loose ends in that case. I learned they were never lured in by Chapman—their rap sheets listed assault and drug charges since their days in juvie court. I eventually lost their trail, thinking they got out of Dodge. But tonight, here they were in Edwards County. I positioned myself to shoot.

"Throw the backpacks in front of you. Now spread your legs and put your hands on top of your head. You're both wanted for attempted murder, drug and human trafficking."

"Really? You're no saint yourself, Nocona Ketemoczy. Scalping someone after shooting them dead. It's like the pot calling the kettle black," laughed Krystal.

Renata never said a word. She kept her eyes on Cooper, threw her backpack in front of her, then spread her legs while putting both hands on top of her head.

"You idiot. He's got nothing on us. We can turn him in for what he did to Lee. I can make an anonymous tip to the FBI right now and big bad border agent is in deep doo-doo. Don't matter if you're a mass murderer in this country, but federal employees got to follow the rules. Might lose their pensions and health benefits," Krystal laughed again.

Renata immediately put her hands down and stepped closer to Krystal.

"We're BFFs, Nocona, although I tell her exactly what to do every single day. Now, call your dog off. We're not going to let him maul us to death and become victims of another one of your weird practices as a border agent," said Krystal.

"If you continue to resist arrest, I will shoot you both," I said, walking around Krystal and Renata, pointing the gun at their backs.

"Get your ass to the truck at the end of this road," I said once I was directly behind them.

Krystal turned around and looked directly at me, inches from my face. And then I saw. Her eyes. They were milky, cloudy, as if she had cataracts. *The Witch of Sonora.* I froze for just a moment in shock, and it took only a minute for life to change forever. She kicked the Maglite out of my hand and reached for the gun.

"Hit him with the flashlight, Renata. Hit him," she screamed.

I could hear Jo screaming my name from the front porch of the house. All I needed was her to drag herself out here, increasing our vulnerability in this mess.

Cooper was jumping on both of them, trying to rip their throats out, as I struggled with Krystal over the gun. Her strength was not that of a mentally and physically depleted girl. It was an unearthly strength, the strength of a witch who feed on human weakness, the weakness of a drug-addicted girl.

"Jesus Christ, girl. I will shoot you dead."

"That Jesus thing. Didn't do too much for your friend Hannah."

I kicked her as hard as I could in the gut, but she didn't let go. Then next thing I knew my world turned black.

When I came to after nearly having my brains bashed in, all was quiet. Cooper was gone. Krystal and Renata were gone. I walked slowly to the house, becoming sicker and sicker with each step, wondering if they had hurt Jo.

Once I was in sight of the front porch, I saw the bodies of Krystal and Renata soaked in their own blood. Jo was sitting on the wooden bench we kept by the front door with a pistol resting on her lap. Cooper sat at her feet with his head low.

"I would have come for you, Noco, but I was busy. Now, I'm just tired. I called Ronnie. He's on his way. Can you help me into the house?"

"You bet."

After we cleaned ourselves up, we collapsed in bed with Cooper at our feet. It was the first time I had let him in our bed, an argument Jo lost to me the first week we lived here. Cooper uttered a content sigh and fell asleep.

"I should have let him sleep with us a long time ago. He's a good dog, Jo. You were right. I should have listened."

"You can't hit a home run every day, Noco, but I say your BA is close to 0.370."

I laughed and held her hand in the dark.

"I wish we didn't have to deal with this."

"Well, we don't have to deal with anything until Ronnie shows up. Let's get some rest while we can. Say goodnight, Noco."

"Goodnight, Noco."

I closed my eyes with a smile on my face, thinking about the woman next to me. My wife, Jo. She was sleeping soundly. There'd be no sleep for me. My head was throbbing from the hit I took, plus my adrenaline was pumping hard, thinking about what went down here in a matter of thirty minutes. But that was life, and the sooner you accepted how fragile it all was, the more you fought to protect it.

My thoughts wandered to Hannah, the other smart and beautiful woman who changed my life. What was the chance of that happening to one man in one lifetime? Luck wasn't the source, didn't have a damn thing to do with it. It was love. Yeah, that same love that made the fortunate get up every morning with smiles on their faces, knowing the world was exploding in a million acts of violence all at once, but they got up anyway. Love made you want to keep giving, keep trying. And I did it every day for the woman beside me. I wasn't letting go.

"Did you hear that, Jo?" I whispered next to her. "I'm never letting you go."

The End

ABOUT THE AUTHOR

Johnnie Bernhard is an award-winning writer whose novels have appeared on notable book lists and awards with *Publisher's Weekly*, *Deep South Magazine*, Kindle Book Awards, the Association of University Presses, Press Women of Texas, and the National Federation of Press Women.

Her novels focus on family, social issues, and the individual's place in an ever-changing world.

A Good Girl was shortlisted in the 2015 William Faulkner-William Wisdom Writing Competition, the 2017 Kindle Book Award for Literary Fiction, and the Mississippi Institute of Arts and Letters Fiction of the Year Award. It was a nominee for the 2018 PEN/Robert W. Bingham Prize and placed in the permanent collection of the Texas State Library and Archive Commission, Texas Center for the Book.

Johnnie's second novel, *How We Came to Be* was named a "Must Read" by *Southern Writers Magazine* and selected for the 2019 *Deep South Magazine* recommended reading list. It is the recipient of the Summerlee Book Prize, HM by the Center for History and Culture at Lamar University.

Her third novel, *Sisters of the Undertow* was chosen for discussion at the 2020 national AWP Conference, the Pat Conroy Literary Center of South Carolina, the Southern Book Festival/Humanities Tennessee, and Words and Music Literary Feast of New Orleans. Named "Best of the University Presses, 100 Books" by the Association of University Presses, *Sisters of the Undertow* was placed in the Texas Center for the Book, State Library Collection and received First Place in the Press Women of Texas Communications Contest. It was named a "Big Texas Read" by Gemini Ink of San Antonio and Writing Workshops of Dallas.

Her fourth novel, *Hannah & Ariela* was named by *Publisher's Weekly Magazine* "Books to Read," May 2022. TCU Press named the novel Best Fiction of 2022 in recognition of University Press Week, Association of University Presses. It was selected as novel of the year by the Press Women of Texas and received First Place, Fiction with the National Federation of Press Women.

Johnnie was chosen as a selected speaker in the 2020 TEDx Fearless Women Series based on her essay, "The Human Story: What Connects Us As Humans Regardless of Geography, Race, and Religion."

She lives in South Texas with her husband.

www.ingramcontent.com/pod-product-compliance
Lightning Source LLC
Jackson TN
JSHW080550130826
106542JS00002B/3
* 9 7 8 1 9 6 5 7 6 6 7 1 2 *